PARANORMAL

HORROR STORIES

True Stories of: Extraterrestrials, UFOs, Demons and Ghost

DAVID M. CURTIS

TABLE OF CONTENTS

INTRODUCTION

Do you remember the moment when you were hooked onto paranormal stories?

I know I do.

My obsession with paranormal began when I was twelve years old. I remember that exact night when my obsession started.

I was sitting on the couch as my parents were watching the evening news, on the TV in the living room. It was a story of a family that was haunted by a spirit of a little girl. What made this story so interesting, was the video footage that the investigators captured.

It was something I had never seen before.

let me remind you this was before the days of YouTube, so video manipulation wasn't as common.

In the video there was a family that was being haunted by the spirit of a little girl. The hauntings where so bad they hired an investigator.

During this investigation there was no children present in the house.

The investigation was taking place in the kitchen, as the camera panned out to the hallway, they catch a glimpse of a girl running across there hallway. As the investigators rush to the hallway they find nothing. This happened a few more times in different areas of the house. You could also hear disembodied voices, and strange knocking.

That footage still gives me chilies till this day, but ever since them I was hooked.

There's something about paranormal stories that fascinate most people including those who don't believe in it.

Despite all the scientific discoveries or paranormal investigations, the fact of the matter is that we have as no clue of what it is.

The urge to know however has always existed and leads us to wanting to find answers. Sometimes people's experiences can hold some clues.

This book is made up of people's real encounters with spirits, apparitions, strange and baffling experiences involving haunted houses, extraterrestrials and UFOs.

The idea behind this book is not to frighten or even prove the existence of the paranormal. It is to simply tell a truthful and realistic account of extraordinary events that were experienced by regular people like you and I.

So, you be the judge. Now site back relax and get ready for Paranormal Horror Stories.

CHAPTER 1:

THE FACEBOOK GHOST

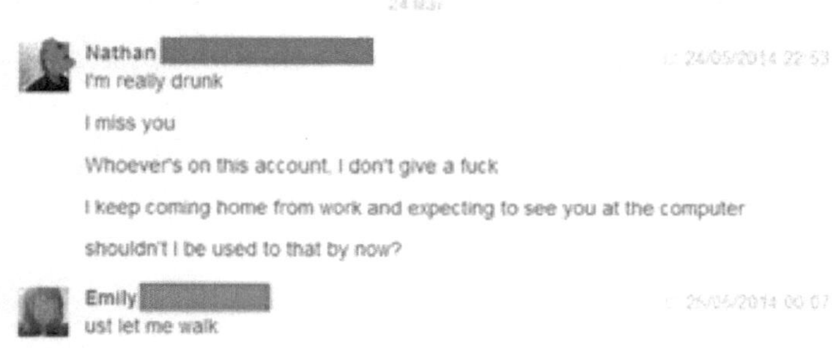

One would imagine that the digital era would be as far removed from the world of ghosts and paranormal phenomena as was possible and one would be wrong. This is the true story of a young man Nathan being haunted by the ghost of his girlfriend Emily, who had tragically perished in a car crash a year before he unexpectedly got to hear from her again. As was to be expected he had missed her terribly and that was all the poignancy the story would have carried had Emily's spirit not reached out to Nathan through her Facebook account seeking help!

Bone chillingly frightening as this may seem all of this occurred according to very precise Facebook timeline details provided by Nathan. It all began when Emily contacted him via her Facebook account in September 2013 with a normal "Hello." Nathan assumed that it was someone else posting on his dead girlfriend's account and posted back demanding to know who the one who was posting was.

He first assumed that it might be Emily's mother who shared admin rights on the account jointly with Nathan or perhaps a friend of his late girlfriend's had hacked her account, but that didn't turn out to be the case. On analyzing Emily's messages, he concluded that these were made of words taken from Facebook chats Emily and he had before the accident occurred. So, he assumed that the message was being sent because of a Facebook programing error.

He got quite concerned however when Emily or whoever was behind what was happening, apparently began tagging herself in his pictures. Bizarrely she would tag herself on his pictures at specific positions where she would have stood next to Nathan had she been alive.

This spooked some of Nathan's friends so much that they unfriended him. Nathan on his part changed Emily's log in details, but the messages would keep coming. He checked with Facebook about the location that the messages were composed, and they turned out to be places she used to be at when she was alive-her mother's place and his.

Things really took an extreme turn on May 8 when Emily sent Nathan her first original message that was at once both heart breaking and very scary. It read *FREEZING*. This was followed a few minutes later by another imploring message read-

 my jumper's in a dryer and it is really cold out

cold

cold

Nathan

Please stop

I'm cold... freezing

I don't know what's happening

Nathan no longer doubted that it was indeed a cold and helpless Emily reaching out to him, imploring for help. As one can imagine, this both terrified and shattered him. He was unable to sleep after reading those messages, and when he did, he had heart-breaking nightmares in which Emily is trapped in a cold and freezing car, even while he is standing warm outside the car shouting at Emily to open the door. She can't seem to hear him, and sometimes her legs seemed to be standing next to Nathan while the rest of the body is inside alluding perhaps to the fact that Emily's body had been severed in the accident.

On May 24 Nathan posted a message for Emily stating that he was drunk and missed her. Her response-

Just let me walk.

Taking that to be a message from her to help set her free, he memorialized Emily's page, hoping that it would provide her with closure. It seemed to work for a short while with Emily going quiet and not even tagging herself on Nathan's pictures as she usually did.

Nathan, in fact, started feeling a little sorry that it was over and was even contemplating killing her page when she got another message from Emily beyond the grave and this time it shook him to the very core of his being. She had sent a picture of him using the computer at his desk which was visible through the latticework of his door. Below the picture was the caption FREEZING.

Nathan was last reported trying to beat a hasty retreat from his home, where he was alone and head to a friend's home, scared out of his mind! Now you may have heard many a scary ghost story that centered on a haunted house or cemetery, but never would you have imagined the premier social media site for the world giving you the chills!

One could of course always discount any of what has been reported in this story and hold that this is all made up, but the fact of the matter is that Nathan put up the details of his very personal account along with screenshots of the relevant Facebook posts on Reddit. Somebody pulling a fast one was hardly likely to so meticulously put up stuff about their private life for public scrutiny like this.

For all those who thought Facebook was a cool place to hang out with friends and share innocent pictures and recipes it sure can spring many a surprise from time to time-even a downright paranormal one! Come to think of it the digital world with its alternative persona and virtual reality facets is very fertile ground for paranormal experiences. Judging from the comments in the online space in response to the Reddit posting by Nathan, regular social media users have been horribly spooked by this post with some claiming that they would now find it difficult to sleep!

People have begun to talk about downloading their persona onto a digital format after they die so that they live on in the virtual world. If that isn't a paranormal phenomenon, then what is? In fact, the digital world is creating an alternate universe of reality, which may one day subsume who we are in the real world and take over. The paranormal will then truly become normal.

CHAPTER 2:

RESURRECTION MARY

Imagine driving down a road in the dead of night, when suddenly, the headlights of the car linger on a figure in front of you. They paint a glimpse of a woman wandering down the middle of the road. You immediately pump the breaks, horrified by the idea of running someone over. Your heart races in your chest, but she's gone. Only the empty asphalt lies in front of you. You try to reassure yourself, to blame it on road fatigue, but you can't shake the image from your mind. Now, imagine actually hitting someone with your car, only to find once again, no one was there. For a stretch of road called Archer Avenue, these instances needed no imagination.

Archer Avenue is a road spanning past the Willowbrook Ballroom and Resurrection Cemetery in the small town of Justice, Illinois. The stretch between the Ballroom and the Cemetery has given rise over the years to a persistent story of a ghostly, hitchhiking apparition that has stalked the road since the 1930's.

This notorious figure was dubbed "Resurrection Mary." She has been described by witnesses as a pretty young girl with blonde hair and a willowy figure. She is said to hitchhike at night. When picked up by drivers, she usually asks to be driven to the Resurrection Cemetery, where, according to multiple witnesses, she simply vanishes into thin air. The details of her appearance are almost perfectly universal in all eyewitness accounts. Her attire is generally made up of a white party dress and dancing shoes. Occasionally smaller details include a clutch purse and a shawl.

Since the thirties, Resurrection Mary has become one of the most infamous paranormal stories in Chicago. Many motorists have given their accounts to reporters, locals, and even police in the town. Such stories in particular have been collected for decades by a man named Richard Crowe. Over the years, he has collected thirty-six accounts which he has deemed substantiated and credible.

The most fascinating stories in his collection involve the drivers who picked up and transported Resurrection Mary. In those stories, motorists met the woman in one of two ways. They either encountered her along the road and offered her a ride, or they met her at one of the nearby dance halls where she would ask them to give her a lift home.

The first recorded encounter with Resurrection Mary began the second way. In 1939, Jerry Palus was on a night out at Liberty Grove and Hall, one of his preferred dance halls. There he met a beautiful young woman who seemed rather reserved and uncommunicative. Despite her quiet nature, Jerry found himself spellbound by the sight of her. He mustered up the courage to approach her and asked her to dance. To his delight, the woman agreed.

He enjoyed hours in her company, but during the night Jerry began to notice some strange things about her. Aside from her distant personality, the young woman's skin was frigid to the touch. Later on in the evening, after a momentary kiss, he noted the same cold rigidness lingered on her lips. Eventually, the woman asked if he would drive her home. Jerry agreed. Soon, the two of them were driving northward on Archer Avenue.

As the car was coming up on Resurrection Cemetery, the girl asked Jerry to pull over to the edge of the road. Even though he thought it was an odd request, Jerry did as she asked. The woman told him that it was time for her to get out of the car. In the darkness, all he could see was the cemetery. Confused, Jerry offered to walk her across the street. She quickly protested and told him that where she was going, he could not follow. Perplexed, Jerry didn't even get to reply before the young lady left the vehicle and walked swiftly towards the gates of the cemetery. Jerry watched her, only to see her disappear in plain sight a few moments later.

Sometime after that incident, Jerry paid a visit to the house at the address the girl had given him at the dance hall. When he got there, he learned that the woman who lived there had lost her daughter a few years earlier.

Another more recent incident was reported by a driver in the summer of 1976. In addition to eyewitness accounts, material evidence was also involved. A driver who was traveling past the cemetery early in the night saw a young woman in the cemetery. She lingered behind the gates and wore Resurrection Mary's signature white dress. The driver didn't stop, but the worry that the girl may have been locked inside the gates tugged at his mind. He made a quick stop in Justice and told the police what he had seen.

Soon after the driver's report, a police officer was sent to investigate the cemetery. When the officer entered, he was unable to find anyone. However, he did take a closer look at the gates. In one particular spot, the bars were bent and looked like they had been scorched by intense heat. The scorch marks he saw were in the shape of handprints. The detail of the bars made local news. Soon scores of curious people descended upon the location to see it with their own eyes. Tourist photos were taken, clearly showing the damage that had been left behind.

The cemetery's management quickly issued a statement explaining that the damage was caused by a service truck that had been deployed to work on the cemetery's sewage system. They explained that the scorch marks had been left by personnel using blowtorches to try and straighten out the bent bars, not by any ghosts. The statement did very little to dissuade people. The cemetery ultimately decided to cut out the disfigured piece of the gate in hopes that people would stop flocking to the cemetery.

In 1979 Bill Geist, a columnist for a Chicago newspaper, did a piece where he interviewed a taxi driver named Ralph about his own encounter with Resurrection Mary.

Ralph stated he was taking the Archer Avenue on a particularly treacherous December night. The weather was cold with rain pouring down in tandem with sleet. Because of the terrible conditions, the cab driver was shocked to see a woman by the road close to the Willowbrook Ballroom. She was walking along the road, scantily clothed in a white dress and a thin shawl. Her outfit seemed ludicrous considering the winter storm swirling around them.

As soon as he caught up to her, Ralph pulled over and offered the poor, drenched girl a ride. She accepted and climbed into the backseat. The driver asked where she wanted to be taken. He told her that he wouldn't charge her the fare. The girl gave vague instructions and simply told him to drive along Archer. Ralph recalled her being reserved and somewhat strange. Under the circumstances, he suspected that she might have been under the influence. The young woman ignored most of his attempts at small talk. She only sporadically mumbled unrelated things.

When the car was passing the cemetery, the girl suddenly started yelling, "Here!" Ralph quickly pulled over to the side of the road. Confused, he tried to figure out why she would want to stop there. As he started to tell the girl that the graveyard was no place to exit the car, he caught a glimpse of the backseat in his rearview mirror. It was empty. Ralph stared in disbelief. The door hadn't opened, but the girl was gone. Ralph professed his shock to Geist in the interview, saying, "May the good Lord strike me dead. It never opened!"

Geist later gave his own comments, particularly concerning Ralph, saying that the man was neither stupid nor crazy. He described him as a completely normal, fifty-two-year-old working man, who was a veteran, father, baseball coach, and a church-going man.

Mary was said to have been spotted in Harlow's nightclub in 1973 twice. Witnesses reported a girl dressed as Resurrection Merry dancing at the club all alone. No one was able to recall her entering the club or explain how she got there, despite the fact that the club checked the ID's of all of their customers.

There was another instance that involved multiple witnesses who believed they saw Mary in 1980. Around twelve eyewitnesses—including the deacon of a local Greek church—reported seeing the spirit on Archer Avenue. Some people even called the police, but they weren't able to hunt down the ghost. Witnesses signaled to the arriving patrols where they had just seen the girl, but there was no longer any sign of Resurrection Mary.

The encounters described above are only some of the reported incidents. Sightings were rampant during the '70's and '80's, but the reports decreased towards the turn of the century. Though the sightings are not as frequent now, they do continue to this day. The legend of Resurrection Mary refuses to die.

Just as her spirit haunts the side of the road, the nature of her identity haunts the minds of those who have come into contact with her tale. Who was Resurrection Mary? Or perhaps a better question would be 'who is Mary?'

A considerable amount of research has been done over the decades in the hopes of uncovering the origins of Justice's local ghost. Regional stories have accumulated since the 1930s, and they have morphed into a widely accepted theory concerning Resurrection Mary's origins. The theory states that a girl was spending time at the Willowbrook Ballroom with her boyfriend. They were dancing and having a pleasant time for the most part until an argument broke out between the two. Angered, the girl left all by herself and stormed outside into the cold. She headed home on foot along Archer Avenue but was hit by a car. The driver fled the scene and was never caught. Her parents buried her at Resurrection Cemetery dressed in her white dress, still wearing her dancing shoes.

Research produced three candidates for the identity of Resurrection Mary: Mary Bregovy, Mary Miskowski, and Anna Marija Norkus. Bregovy and Miskowski both died in car accidents in 1934 and 1930, respectively. Anna Marija Norkus perished in an accident in 1927. All three of the unfortunate girls were buried at Resurrection Cemetery.

Bregovy died during the first half of the 1930's which would make sense in the ghost's timeline; however, there are certain details that do not fully support the legend of Resurrection Mary. When Bregovy was killed, she was nowhere near Willowbrook. She was killed in downtown Chicago. Her death was also not a hit-and-run accident, but rather a car crash involving the vehicle she was in. Bregovy's appearance did not match that of the reported ghost either. She had short, black hair, and she was buried in different clothes than the ones worn by Resurrection Mary. As for Miskowski, not much is known about her, except that she was killed in a traffic accident in 1930 while crossing the street to get to a Halloween party. That information alone is not enough to go on, leaving the possibility of Miskowski being the spirit inconclusive.

The supposed connection between Anna Norkus and Resurrection Mary became the most popular as years went by. Ursula Bielski, an author from Chicago, conducted some thorough research with a friend in 1999 concerning the connection. Anna Norkus, who later in life started using the middle name of "Marija/Maria," was killed when she left the ballroom and headed home in July of 1927. The girl was only twelve at the time of her death. She was blonde, slim, and quite grown for her age. Her description aligned perfectly with the eyewitness accounts of the ghost. She also loved to dance and persuaded her father to take her to the ballroom that fateful night.

In the story that Bielski published, there were very little contradictions by those who encountered the ghost. There are, however, some discrepancies between the findings and the legend of Mary's origins. Who is to say though that some of the folklore hasn't been muddied up and disfigured over time? After all, the original story of a couple's argument where the girl wandered into the night is just that – a local legend developed over the decades. The biggest difference is the fact that Anna Norkus died in a car crash as her father was driving her home that night, not in a hit-and-run.

While it's unlikely that the ghost's actual backstory will ever be determined beyond a reasonable doubt, that won't stop the witnesses from speculating or keep Resurrection Mary from making her nighttime appearances. So, to those who traverse the notorious stretch of Archer Avenue at night, keep your wits about you and your eyes on the road ahead. You never know who you might run into.

CHAPTER 3:
PRESIDENTIAL ENCOUNTERS WITH EXTRATERRESTRIALS

Many people across the United States believe that their government is aware of the existence of extraterrestrials; that they are more than just aware of their existence, but in fact, have interacted with them in one way or another. Some even believe the US government has signed agreements or treaties with otherworldly individuals. This, of course, would involve leaders of the country, particularly the United States presidents who have come and gone into office over the years; though some of these individuals had strange encounters or experiences well before serving their terms.

For the skeptic, consider this: is it not a striking coincidence that multiple presidents have reported various kinds of encounters with unidentified flying objects and possible "aliens?" These people are entrusted with the wellbeing of the country and occupy positions of not just power but also great responsibility. Coming forth with this kind of information could be viewed as "crazy" or "unstable;" or simply discredit their ability to perform as needed for the United States. Why volunteer this information in view of such large associated risk? Coincidence or not, it certainly is interesting and thought-provoking, as well as curious and shrouded in mystery.

Before his presidential reign, Jimmy Carter had a notable encounter in Georgia, which he recounted to an audience on *Larry King Live*. In the year of '69 during his presidential campaign (as governor) he, along with approximately 25 other men, witnessed a strange object in the sky. He described it as a strange, round light appearing in the Western sky and headed towards the group of men. It grew closer and closer, stopping and hovering just above some towering pine trees, where it began to change color, switching from blue, to red, then white. It stayed in this state for a while (though a specific length of time was not disclosed) and then disappeared. According to Mr. Carter, everyone who witnessed the event was "aghast". There is an official documented report on this incident that has also been corroborated by over 10 other individuals who witnessed the scene.

President Carter said he initially never thought of it as an alien-inhabited unidentified flying object, as he simply didn't think it was possible for aliens to visit Earth from other planets. He *did* request NASA, though, to investigate unidentified flying objects during his presidency in the year 1977. He also announced to the public that should he be elected as president of the United States, he would make available to the public all information possessed by the US about unidentified flying objects and extraterrestrials. He later said that he was certain unidentified flying objects exist because he had, in fact, seen one (referencing this event). It was unfortunate, however, that despite the request for an investigation from the United States president, which is regarded as the highest form of power and service in office, NASA still declined.

The 1970's seem to be a significant decade for unidentified flying objects and possible extraterrestrial encounters. In 1977, President Ronald Reagan may have had a visual encounter with an alien craft. This encounter was narrated by Mr. Reagan's companion at that time, a pilot by the name of Bill Paynter. The pilot narrated that he was flying with Ronald Reagan aboard (as well as other individuals that were unnamed) when they suddenly saw a large light following behind their plane. The light then quickly accelerated with great speed; and after following it for a few minutes, they saw it ascend upwards until it was completely gone. The pilot did not file an official report but has been quoted by certain publications as saying that he and President Ronald Reagan often discussed the unidentified flying objects encounter.

Another striking possible encounter was reported to President Thomas Jefferson in the year 1813. This was long before the other reported incidences when technology was even more limited, and thus, flying objects were a rarity. This report was made to President Jefferson via a letter written by two men, one of whom was a carpenter. The letter revealed details about an encounter they had in Portsmouth, Virginia; describing a large object that seemingly looked like a ball of fire, surrounded by smoke that was being emitted from itself. The object was then concealed for several minutes by this very same smoke. When it was visible again, it appeared to change shape, shifting from a round form to that of a more elongated oblong or "turtle" outline. The object continually fluctuated about in the sky, all the while emitting enormous amounts of smoke. It was seen descending downward, and then reascending up to its previous height. There is no feasible explanation as to what this may have been, especially during that time. There is no feasible explanation as to what this may have been, especially during that time period. The possibilities are very limited, and as such, it was truly an unidentified flying object.

President John F. Kennedy was famous for a lot of things; though you probably did not know that he is closely intertwined with unidentified flying object sightings and the possible existence of extraterrestrials. An author by the name of William Lester says he discovered a top-secret memo from

President John Kennedy to the CIA that had just recently been declassified and made available to the public. In his book, he disclosed the details of this memo, stating that it was a request from the President for the CIA to organize all of their files regarding unidentified flying objects and to debrief him on all these unknown occurrences. Said memo, Lester said, was dated November 12th of the year 1962. This would put such request by JFK just 10 days before his tragic death. The authenticity of this top-secret memo, however, is under question, as it has not been located anywhere outside of Lester's own records and his book. Was it deleted to hide a trail that could lead to ground-breaking information on Earth's encounters with extraterrestrials? Or was it entirely fabricated by an author to substantiate his own claims?

There are numerous conspiracy theories that involve President John Kennedy, but no concrete evidence has been found to support these theories and claims. There is, however, a report of a certain letter sent to JFK by a woman, detailing her own personal encounter with what may have been an alien-piloted unidentified flying object that she had seen through a bedroom window in her home located in Ashland, Wisconsin. Though the file does not contain the original letter to Mr. Kennedy, it does have other documents, such as the report of an official letter sent to the woman printed on a Department of the Air Force letterhead. In this letter, which was dated July 23 of the year 1962, it was stated that the presidential office had asked the US Air Force to reply to her with regards to the "unidentified serial lighting" seen from her bedroom window. This response to the woman included a letter and a questionnaire from Lt. Colonel William J. Lockadoo, United States Air Force, for the woman to fill out and return. Unfortunately, the questionnaire was filled in with pencil and the print is no longer readable on the copies found on file. Many people suspect that the original letter written by the woman to President Kennedy, as well as his response to her, was purposely removed from the file. Is it possible that these missing documents contained some shocking information?

Whether you were (or would have been) on board with President Richard M. Nixon and his particular brand of leadership, he is perhaps the first president to publicly acknowledge that he was being briefed on the subject of extraterrestrial unidentified flying objects. However, he also said he was "not at liberty to discuss" any government knowledge of such things.

At the Citizen Hearing on Disclosure held by the National Press Club in 2013, a former CIA and Army employee volunteered information in which he confirmed that Richard Nixon and another president (Dwight Eisenhower) both knew that alien spacecraft was being secretly held in New Mexico, all the way back since the 1950's. This former employee also stated that both he and his CIA superior were told by President Eisenhower and then Vice-President

Richard Nixon to work for confirmation that the stories surrounding Area 51 were more than just rumors and were, in fact, accurate.

What is drastically more intriguing than the possibility of witnessing alien spacecraft is the possibility of actually seeing the lifeless remains of extraterrestrials from the Roswell crash. This is another reportedly true event experienced by President Richard Nixon and his friend, Jackie Gleason. This incident was recounted by Beverly Gleason Mckittrick, Mr. Gleason's former wife. Beverly stated, on several occasions during interviews, that Jackie Gleason had come home late one night in the year 1973, seeming to be quite shaken-up about something. He reportedly told her that he had been taken to see Mr. Nixon, who escorted him to Homestead Air Force base. He then proceeded to show Gleason the deceased bodies of small aliens that were being housed there. This same story, with the same information, was retold by Beverly in an interview as recently as 2003, during which she also added that she took him at his word because he had been very serious about the incident when he recounted it to her. She also said that releasing the information had put quite a strain on their marriage, as he was very angry with her for doing so. It is widely known that Mr. Nixon and Mr. Gleason were good friends, and they were often seen golfing together. Is this why President Nixon entrusted Jackie Gleason with this sensitive sight and information?

CHAPTER 4:

THE PATERSON FAMILY POSSESSION

Possession is a particularly unsettling phenomenon for certain people. For those who believe that possessions do happen and who investigate them, there is a fine line between insanity and actual demons. To an untrained and fresh eye, this line can be rather hard to see, but there are some cases where there appears to be a line so clear that it becomes almost undeniable. This holds especially true for those stories where credible and official reports corroborate the events. Case in point: The Paterson family.

The events that transpired at the Paterson family home in Toledo, Ohio toed the line between superstition and belief until it crossed into the documented unknown. The trouble began in November of 2011, shortly after Ann Paterson—a single mother of three—moved into a new house with her children and her mother, Janet Green. Unfortunately for the Paterson family, they soon found out that they were not alone.

Despite the cold, November weather, large numbers of flies swarmed towards the house. No matter how many insects the family killed, the flies kept coming. Late at night when the family was tucked away in their beds, footsteps would creak and echo as if someone were pacing up the stairs leading from the dark basement to the kitchen. The strange occurrences didn't stop there. The hordes of insects and mysterious sounds were only the beginning.

A chilling sight appeared in the home one day. A horrifying apparition of a male figure walked through the family's living room. Upon seeing the specter, Rosa rushed forward to try and investigate, but when she got closer, no one was there. Believing that the sighting had simply been a trick of the light would have been all too easy, except for one thing: The figure had left behind a trail of wet footprints.

As disturbing as those occurrences were, things soon moved from eerie to potentially dangerous. Four months after the family had moved in, the malicious nature of the haunting began to reveal itself. On the night of March 10th, the family was up late grieving the passing of someone they were close to. Around two in the morning, a cry rang out in the home. Rosa raced to her granddaughter's room where Ann was screaming in panic.

Upon entering the room, Rosa was shocked to see her twelve-year-old granddaughter levitating above the bed.

Terror rooted them in place. Rosa, Ann, and several friends that had been visiting the mourning family broke out in prayer. Under the petrifying circumstances, it was the only thing they could think of to do. Soon after the prayers started, the young girl fell back into her bed. She woke up from a trance-like state, visibly confused and unaware of what had just transpired.

After the levitation, the two women were convinced that an evil presence had taken up residence in their home. Ann and her mother agreed to seek out help. They made contact with one of the churches in the area, whose officials concluded that malicious ghosts were occupying the house. The two women also contacted seers. The mediums confirmed what the women had already suspected: there were actual demons haunting the family. Taking the advice they were given, Ann and Rosa used olive oil to protect the children from further possession. Ann also constructed an altar in the basement of the house. After following prescribed measures in the hopes of cleansing the house of unwanted spirits, the family was blessed with a few days of normalcy. However, the lull in activity was not to last.

Soon, the family's torment began again—this time with increased intensity. Odd behavior manifested in the children. They began acting up and becoming increasingly malicious. Ann became convinced that demons had possessed her three kids. The possessions seemed to manifest in random outbursts. Unsettling things began to happen to the children. Their eyes would roll back or bulge in their sockets, they would smirk eerily like they were plotting to do harm, and strange pitch changes plagued their voices. At one point, Ann's youngest son was found hiding in the closet, talking to someone that wasn't there. At first it was thought that the boy had an imaginary friend, but when he was questioned about it, the boy said that he had been talking to another boy who was describing what death was like to him.

There were times when the haunting became so dangerous that the family was forced to relocate temporarily to hotels. Things had moved past being mentally disturbing and had begun to manifest in physically harmful ways. At one point, the seven-year-old boy was thrown out of the bathroom by a formidable, unseen force. On another occasion, the twelve-year-old girl was injured and required stitches.

Things were quickly becoming too much for the family to bear. They decided to consult their physician, Dr. Stewart, and have the children examined. Ann explained everything that she and her family were going through. He told reporters that he found the story very disturbing. It was a tale unlike any other in his career. In his reports, he later wrote that the family was suffering from hallucinations and delusions of ghosts.

During the visit to the doctor, the possession manifested again. The event was later covered in a Department of Child Services report after the agency became involved. Reportedly, the children lashed out at Stewart. Ann's sons cursed at the man in inexplicably deranged voices. The doctor's medical staff reported that the Paterson' youngest son flew up into the air and smashed into a wall—without any interference from anyone present. At that point, both boys lost consciousness. The doctor's staff phoned for emergency services out of concern for the children. Police officers and ambulances arrived at the scene shortly.

Both boys were transported to the local hospital in Toledo, Ohio. When they regained consciousness, the seven-year-old flew into a highly disturbed and out of control tantrum. The child exhibited such impossible strength that it took multiple personnel to restrain him. It soon became apparent to the medical staff that there was something wrong with the children, and the Department of Child Services was called. The DCS was brought in to investigate the situation. Suspicions of possible child abuse and concerns that Ann may have been suffering from a mental disorder began to swirl around the family. Even though the concerned caller was not named, the DCS reports do mention that the anonymous source believed that Ann made her children perform the incidents to support her story about possession.

Valerie Washington was assigned to manage the Paterson case and investigate the allegations. As part of this task, she also gave a statement to the police concerning that day. Valerie explained that Ann and the children were examined for injuries and any other ailments. All of them appeared to be healthy at the time. Ann also underwent a psychiatric evaluation and was ruled to be of sound body and mind.

When Valerie spoke to the family while still at the hospital, the younger son continued to act in a bizarre fashion. The boy growled with his teeth bared like an animal while his eyes rolled back. At one point, he even lunged at his older brother and tried to strangle him before being forcibly dragged off of the older boy.

Later on, a hospital nurse accompanied Rosa and Valerie into a special room where they were to conduct further interviews and examinations with the boys. Once again, the younger boy began to growl at his brother, but it didn't stop there. In a very unsettling voice, the young boy told his brother, "It's time to die." Meanwhile, the older boy started bashing his head against his grandmother. As disturbing as the violence was, it was nothing compared to what happened next.

With a terrifying grin plastered on his face, the older boy walked up the wall backwards. His feet stuck to the wall and the ceiling. Still smiling dementedly, he flipped over his grandmother and landed directly on his feet. This incident was documented in Valerie's official report for the DCS and confirmed by nurse Walker. Police questioned Valerie about the incident, and she said that the boy "glided" his way up the wall to the ceiling. She also said that both she and Walker fled from the room, horrified by what they had witnessed. Her account of the incident was filed in a police report, as well as her own report for the DCS.

Valerie's personal report further stated that the doctor at the hospital was informed of the incident, but he didn't believe it. When the doctor asked the boy to repeat his demonic stunt as proof, the child was confused and didn't remember the act. It was at that point that Valerie indicated that there was indeed the possibility of an "evil influence" at play.

That night, Ann stayed at the hospital with her youngest son while her mother took the rest of the children to a relative's house in town. The next day, on the youngest son's eighth birthday, Rosa was called by the DCS to bring her granddaughter and grandson back to the hospital for further investigation. As things turned out, the DCS officials had made the decision to seize custody over the children for the time being. Valerie informed Ann of the emergency decision, but she reassured the single mother that it was most likely only temporary. Valerie also noted in her report that the children were in distress—whether it was from being separated from their mother or part of the possession, their suffering was undeniable.

Not long after the events, the hospital chaplain called a priest named Michael Maginot. The chaplain asked him to try and exorcise a demon out of Ann's older son. The Catholic Church took the matter of exorcism very seriously. Michael informed the chaplain that he would need his bishop's permission before agreeing to such an undertaking. However, Michael did agree to conduct an interview with Ann and Rosa at their home.

The interview lasted for a few hours and left Michael with the belief that the family was indeed haunted by demons. According to the priest and the women, there was no shortage of paranormal occurrences in the home during their conversation. Lights would flicker and stop as soon as approached, window blinds moved on their own, and the mysterious wet footprints made another appearance. Michael also witnessed Ann's convulsive reaction when he exposed her to his crucifix. After a few hours of consulting about the other paranormal events that the family had been plagued with, the priest blessed the home and left. He advised the women to leave as well. Rosa and Ann heeded his advice and relocated to a relative's house for a while.

A few days later, however, Ann and Rosa were called back to the house for a DCS inspection of the conditions of the home. Valerie Washington—accompanied by a police officer from Lake County—conducted the inspection. They were joined by two more policemen who were curious about the happenings at the Paterson family home—one was from the Gary police department, and the other was from the department in Hammond.

When the group arrived at the house, Ann was hesitant to go inside. Rosa stepped up and took everyone in by herself. One of the officers, Austin, who tagged along from the local police department said that he harbored a certain dose of belief in the supernatural in general. He was however, highly skeptical of the existence of demons specifically. After visiting the family's house, Austin's opinion began to change.

According to official police reports from the officers present, a number of peculiar things happened during their stay. Electronics behaved strangely. Fresh batteries drained and suddenly went dead. Audio recorders failed at random intervals. Voice recorders registered strange noises that sometimes took on the form of disembodied voices.

The officer from Lake County took routine photos while on site, only to find that the photos contained some strange phenomena. Spots, smears, and shapes that looked like ghostly figures haunted the images. The images were documented in his official report. Austin, the local cop, took photos with his smartphone. His photos showed similar disturbances. Austin also reported that strange occurrences followed him home. His patrol car's radio experienced interference, and his home's garage door refused to open. No malfunction or power outage was discovered.

After the inspection, the Department of Child Services was granted indefinite custody over Ann's children on various grounds. The kids reportedly skipped out on school frequently, which Ann stated was due to illnesses and exhaustion brought on by the demons. The children were separated while in DCS custody. The youngest boy was sent to Wheatfield for observation and psychiatric examinations. The other two were put in a foster care center in Chicago.

Even though the youngest son was found to be healthy, he was still exhibiting strange behavior akin to possession. However, these instances only seemed to arise when subject of demons was brought up. The psychiatrist who evaluated him concluded that he was not psychotic, but simply taught by his mother and relatives to act that way.

The other two children underwent evaluations as well. During conversations with psychiatrists, Ann's daughter maintained that she had seen ghostly apparitions in her house and experienced trances. Her brother also spoke of strange phenomena, such as doors slamming and household items moving on their own. Separate evaluations of both children concluded that what was at work was, by all indications, an elaborate delusion. The same conclusion was drawn in most of Ann's psychiatric evaluations, as well.

Regardless, Ann and the rest of the family stuck to their belief that demons were upon them. The Department of

Child Services established a plan for Ann, which consisted of multiple points concerning her relationship with the children. She was to find a job, among other things, in order to work towards getting her children back. The Paterson children were still to remain in DCS custody for the time being.

In the period that followed, officers and DCS caseworkers continued their investigations into the family's house. The initial group now accompanied by Reverend Michael Maginot and two more Lake County cops. They visited the house again, supported by another DCS case manager named Samantha Ilic. Samantha replaced Valerie because she refused to enter the home again.

While Samantha was unconvinced of the existence of demons, she reported having strange sensations while in the house. At one point, she thought she suffered a panic attack. Difficulty breathing forced her to go outside. Some of the cops also reported something particularly strange that day.

In the bedroom, they witnessed an oily liquid trickling down the blinds on the window. They were unable to determine the source. The officers conducted their own test to determine whether something paranormal was at play with this strange substance. One of them wiped the oil off of the blinds with a paper towel. The officers then left the room, but they stayed outside for around twenty-five minutes and made sure no one else went in. Police records state that surely enough, the liquid appeared once again when they entered the room a second time. The priest was certain that this was a sign of the demons. Convinced of the possession, Michael asked his bishop for permission to conduct an exorcism on Ann.

The bishop was initially reluctant to allow a full exorcism, so the reverend first performed a minor ritual. This rite lasted for around two hours and was witnessed by the caseworker, Ilic, as well as two police officers. Ilic reported that she indeed felt a foreign presence during the ritual, although she still wouldn't concede to it being of demonic nature.

Eventually, Michael was given permission for a major exorcism. He conducted three exorcisms on Ann by June 2012. All of the rituals except the very last one were witnessed by the police officers, who were there to provide any assistance the priest may have needed. Throughout the rituals, Ann said she experienced immense pain and struggle. She compared the ordeal to giving birth.

After the final and most intense exorcism, which the priest performed in Latin, it appeared as though things were taking a turn for the better. Ann and the reverend parted ways. Sometime after these excruciating trials—around six months after the DCS took custody of Ann's children—the family was reunited. The children were returned to their mother on the basis that the family was moving past the experience—for the most part. The three children and their mother were all joyous at the reunion and managed to move on with their lives.

As far as Ann Paterson was concerned, it was God, not the psychiatrists, who helped her family move forward. Even though a child walking backwards onto a ceiling sounds like something straight out of "The Exorcist," the amount of official reports on the incident should also be taken into consideration. One can only wish that Ann had been the only witness so that she could be easily dismissed, but—unpleasantly for us—she was far from alone. Whatever the actual cause for the disturbances, one thing is certain: this was an all but routine case for the Department of Child Services.

CHAPTER 5:

CANADIAN GOVERNMENT AND THEIR KNOWLEDGE OF EXTRATERRESTRIALS AND UFOS

While there are a number of profound reports on unidentified flying objects and possible extraterrestrial encounters in the United States, it does not have a corner on the market for this type of incident. Canada, the friendly next-door neighbor of America, has its fair share of encounters as well. In fact, it is contributing quite a bit to the growing number of declassified reports vis-a-vis unidentified flying objects. There have been a number of documents released that indicate the Canadian government's role in the unidentified flying object and extraterrestrial research.

There are 6 detailed reports in the recently disclosed documents, all made by Wing Commander Douglas Robertson, that discusses possible unidentified flying object and alien encounters. These reports were made in the year 1966; and, curiously enough, the incidence of reported unidentified flying object sightings went up by four hundred percent from the year '66 to '67. This may be why the Canadian government began taking a serious interest in this kind of event.

The Canadian government sorts this type of report into one of several categories that they believe pertain to the incident at hand, based on the initial written report as well as interviews and assessment of the individuals involved. These categories include: hoaxes, psychological hysteria (or mass hysteria), naturally occurring phenomena that is misconstrued, military-related events, psychological illness or misconception due to psychological state; and finally, sightings and events that do not fit into any category but are truly considered legitimate unknown events, or unidentified (as in UFO). One of these reports includes not just Canada's most notable unidentified flying object incident, but is also often regarded as the most profound worldwide: The "Falcon Lake Incident".

Near Falcon Lake, Manitoba, in the late spring of May 1967, a man by the name of Stefan Michalak was prospecting when he spotted something peculiar in the sky. Hovering just ahead of him were two luminescent objects. He then observed one of the two objects accelerate away, while the other made a landing nearby, about 150 feet away. Mr. Michalak described the object as a "craft" that appeared silver in color and about 35 feet in diameter. He also stated it was brightly and intensely lit. He further reported that he slowly approached the unknown craft and was just reaching a proximity close enough for him to be able to touch it, when the craft revved up and accelerated away, knocking and landing him on his back in the process. This is quite a statement already, but things didn't stop here for this particular reported incident.

After the incident, Mr. Michalak began suffering from ill health over the course of a few short weeks. He began to experience headaches, nausea, vomiting, weight loss, blackouts, and memory loss, all of which were consistent with symptoms of radiation toxicity. After examining him thoroughly, doctors were at a loss. They could not find anything wrong that would explain Stefan's condition.

Nine months passed with no answers when another health issue arose. He collapsed and then discovered strange burn marks in a grid-like pattern on his chest. Upon this new incident, his doctor decided more diagnostic tests should be performed on his patient; so he was sent to the Mayo Clinic. After a few weeks, when his referring doctor attempted to follow up on the testing performed at the Mayo Clinic, there was somehow no record of a Stefan Michalak as a patient, let alone any test result. The entirety of this strange encounter is well-documented, corroborated, and substantiated, which lend credibility and contribute to this being one of the most remarkable incidents on file. The declassified documents reveal that there were signs and indications of radioactivity involved in this particular case; yet, there are no explanations for it and no resolution has been found.

Lesser known, but still documented, cases include strange radar sightings and photos of unknown craft or unidentified flying objects. The very fact that the Canadian government has delved into researching unidentified flying objects leads to a lot of questions and speculations. In fact, multiple organizations and agencies became involved in this investigation and research, starting with the Department of National Defense. The Royal Canadian Mounted Police took part in the year 1947, when they began receiving numerous reports on unidentified objects in the sky. It was then that they started to officially collect information and compile documents on unidentified flying objects.

In 1950, a scientist and engineer by the name of Wilbert Smith began work on a project dubbed "Project Magnet," in conjunction with the Department of Transport. The primary purpose of this group was to study magnetic phenomena, with the idea that the Earth's magnetic field could be manipulated and used as a way of propelling spacecraft and vehicles. Mr. Smith was noted as already believing the technology was already in existence and being used by the unidentified flying objects that were so often seen in the Canadian skies. Project Second Story followed the formation of Project Magnet in the year 1952, sponsored by the Defense

Research Board. This project's sole purpose was to assess and evaluate all reports of unidentified flying craft or "saucers".

In 1959, Canada and the United States agreed upon an arrangement for a joint reporting system for unidentified flying objects. During this time, information was disseminated to make the public aware. This information stated that any and all "hostiles" appearing suspicious, or all unidentified craft that was seen, should be immediately reported. As expected, by 1961, the Department of National Defense was receiving numerous reports of unidentified flying objects. When the Royal Canadian Mounted Police were questioned on their stand regarding the matter, they stated that they maintained an open-minded stance and that every reported incident was investigated. This additional acknowledgment and statement further fuelled even back then, the belief that the Canadian government may be holding substantial evidence on an extraterrestrial and alien craft activity.

CHAPTER 6:

THE AMAZING TRUE REED FAMILY STORY OF ALIEN ENCOUNTER

It was very difficult to include a verifiable true alien encounter story, far more difficult than the UFO encounter story for the obvious reason that of all the reported paranormal phenomena this is the least likely to be believed. Most people will declare you a certified nut case if you tell them that you saw an alien.

"Yeah, you must have finally had a look in the mirror. Didn't I always tell you that you looked weird? Now you have proved it. You are weird!

In the 1960s four members of Creed family spanning four generations claimed to have had extremely close encounters with aliens who had in fact even abducted and imprisoned them in their space ship before letting them go. Now that is as bizarre and unbelievable a story you ever heard and could you fault the whole wide world for not believing a word of it?

The Reeds account of what were for them life altering incidents begins in the year 1966, when as a six year old Thomas Reed, living in his family horse farm in the Berkshires is surprised by strange otherworldly lights and figures in the hallway and before he could fully understand what was happening, he finds himself and his younger brother Matthew in the woods close to his home looking up at a UFO.

Astoundingly they are both abducted and taken inside the spacecraft where Thomas remembers being made to see the projection of a willow tree. The next encounter occurs a year later, this time in their Broadman Street home in Sheffield. Thomas remembers seeing more of the bizarre lights he had encountered the last time accompanied this time by the sound of doors banging and yet again he finds himself and his younger brother in the spacecraft. Strangely the next thing he remembers is being picked up from their driveway by his frantic mother who had gone looking for her kids on horseback.

There was to be one more fateful encounter between the Reed family and the aliens two years later in 1969 when Thomas, Matthew, their mother, and grandmother saw some strange lights while going down Route 7. Soon enough their car stalled and the four of them find themselves inside a large room. Thomas, in fact, is taken to meet two grotesque ant like beings after which he is put into a cage. Mercifully he finds himself back in his car soon after that.

Who would believe such a spectacularly bizarre story of the most incredible alien encounter and hardly anybody did. It would have been easier for Thomas to disown the story and avoid the ridicule that came his way in the subsequent decades, but he followed his mother's advice always to speak the truth about what had happened with not very happy consequences for his reputation. In fact, his searing encounters with aliens had left him badly traumatized and suffering from typical symptoms of Post Stress Disorder. Therefore to point fingers at him, when all that he did was recount the truth was absolutely not on. Life sometimes can be terribly unfair to those who have always been fair with the others.

But quite unexpectedly and some would say as strangely as the alleged alien encounters themselves, recognition came from the most unlikely of sources-The Great Barrington Historical Society and Museum. This is really a big deal in the sense that this is a regular historical society that does not impart official status to an event unless there is credible proof of that having occurred.

The fact of the matter was that there were in fact dozens of credible eye witnesses in the area at the time of the reported incident in 1969, who had admitted seeing a disc shaped spacecraft perform what appeared to be very complex maneuvers. Some of them had in fact even called the local Radio Station, WSBS which had then gone on to report on the sightings. The Radio Station handed over the relevant recordings to the society for verification. What also worked in Thomas's favor was the polygraph test he had earlier undertaken, which he had passed with flying colors.

The society, therefore, thought it fit to deem the reported happenings "significant and true." That Thomas Reed's paranormal encounter with aliens had found widespread support and acceptance was proved when local residents raised $5000 and erected a monument to commemorate the momentous event that occurred forty nine years ago.

Sceptics abound though, and some vandal damaged the memorial son after its inauguration, but what is worth noting is that the Reed family have not made any money from their retelling of their extraordinary expenses and for the past many decades suffered only trauma and disdain. If they stuck to their story, it was because they knew that it was the truth. But for some people truth clearly is not enough.

The most brilliant minds of the world like Einstein and Stephen Hawking concede that it is almost certain that alien life exists somewhere in the unfathomably vast universe. Earth is but one planet in our solar system and our solar system, in turn, is one of the billions in our galaxy, The Milky Way. The Milky Way itself is one of the billions of galaxies that populate the universe. Is it then feasible that there won't be life anywhere else?

For those who pride themselves on their logical train of thought would accept that by applying the law of probability of the existence of alien life is very high indeed. Why then is it such a stretch of the imagination to accept that people might be encountering alien life from time to time? One would imagine that with odds for alien life existing being as high as they are, it would be weird if there wasn't some alien-human contact from time to time!

CHAPTER 7:
THE TRUTH ABOUT AREA 51

One of the most well-known alien-related mysteries is, of course, the event that took place in Roswell, New Mexico in 1947; otherwise known as Area 51. The term is used to refer to an area of land that was acquired by the government, although they completely denied its existence until the year 2013. It is so tightly guarded by heavily armed personnel, preventing unwanted entrants or infiltration, that the general consensus is that there is something extremely important being held in secret there. There are so many reports on phenomena surrounding Area 51 that it would be an insurmountable task to discuss them all, but there are some that are especially noteworthy and intriguing.

A former pilot of an airline reported a 1988 incident that has since received quite a lot of attention. While en route to San Francisco, he and his co-pilot were suddenly interrupted by air traffic control. He was told to change course and await further instructions. As the plane was nearing the desert area just outside of Area 51, he saw what seemed to be a strange hologram appearing across the surface of the desert. He stated it was made up of various hues of blue and violet lights that were intersecting at 90-degree angles. He also described something he had never seen before, which he said resembled a "three-dimensional instrument landing system." The stream of light, he said, extended upwards for at least 5 miles high and was a ½ mile across. He then witnessed what he described as approximately 2 dozen "firefly-like" small lights that scattered upward towards the sky, making quick right turns, before accelerating back down into the stream of light. Suddenly, all of these lights simply vanished from his and his co-pilot's sights. As soon as the lights disappeared, air traffic control instructed them to seek another course to San Francisco without any explanation.

Another report about Area 51 is told by a security officer of a nearby mine named Charlie Arrendale, who, in 1965, received some seemingly odd instructions. For two consecutive nights, he was ordered to guard the area and shoot on sight anyone or anything that came near the site. He and some other officers were bussed to and from the area. While on duty the first night, Mr. Arrendale heard a strange, low-frequency humming sound for what he estimated to be about 30 minutes. Immediately after the noise stopped, he and the rest of the security staff were rounded up and transported back out. As they were riding on their way, Charlie witnessed a troop of men surrounding a circular tent that was set up on a runway. He said the men had their backs turned to the strange tent and were all heavily armed. The second night on duty, Charlie heard the same low humming sound as the previous night. This time, though, when it stopped and they were bussed back out, the tent and the troops that were guarding it were not there anymore. Why was there a tent set up on a runway? What was inside? And why did it need to be so heavily guarded?

Two men named Walter Kasza and Robert Frost even lost their lives due to what their widows said were strange events involving Area 51. They were civilian contractors working for the Air Force. In the year 1994, they were on a job and present when some unidentified chemicals were burned for disposal. The exposure resulted in skin, liver, and respiratory illnesses that eventually claimed the lives of the two men. Post-mortem, biopsies of their skin were taken and tested. The results showed the presence of industrial toxins that people do not typically come in contact with. Unfortunately, their widows were never able to get resolution, since Area 51 was exempted from disclosure of such information due to a law granted by then president, Bill Clinton. No answers as to what the chemicals were, or why they were burned, were ever uncovered.

One of the most gripping incidents regarding Area 51 took place in the year 1997 on a radio show called *Coast to Coast*. A man called in to say that he had once worked at Area 51. He sounded genuinely scared and claimed that "extra-dimensional beings" have infiltrated different components of the military. He also said that these beings wanted to "wipe out" heavily populated areas. Unfortunately, the call was interrupted and dropped, which convinced many people that the government was listening in on the call and cut it off to prevent the leak of information.

The theories surrounding Area 51 range from it harboring crashed alien aircraft and deceased alien species, to simply being a facility that the government uses for the development of secret military technology. Nevertheless, the officially released information is that Area 51 was approved by President Eisenhower as a test site. It was referred to as Area 51 due to its location segment on maps. With that said, the Pentagon did eventually confirm that there was a 22 million-dollar government program dedicated specifically to analyzing and evaluating unidentified aerial threats.

CHAPTER 8:
CURSED SISTER

Cindy tells of a few frightening events concerning her younger sister Ashley.

Back when the girls were younger, the family worked at an all-boys summer camp located somewhere on a mountain. Ashley later insisted that the place was haunted. She experienced strange things happening. Objects moved on their own and wet footsteps could be heard. The weirdest part was that she knew the ghost was a girl and that the poor soul had drowned. Since then, Ashley refused to go to the camp.

Years later, the new aquatics director encountered the ghost in the dining hall. She saw the soaking wet girl opening cupboards and trying to push people down the stairs. She also heard her running around at night. They weren't the only ones to have an encounter with the ghost, affirming what Ashley had claimed years prior.

One time, while the camp's manager was fixing a leaky faucet in the men's bathroom, he heard wet footsteps come in. He told the person that he'd be done in a minute, but when he got up, no one was there. All he saw was a puddle of water in the middle of the floor. He had the whole place investigated by a paranormal team which confirmed their suspicions: the place was indeed haunted.

Fast forward to when the sisters are all grown up.

One day, Ashley moved back home after living in Hawaii for a while. She claimed that her former boyfriend was being an abusive, so she left him. Three days after moving back in, things started to get strange. At three in the morning, three fire alarms went off in the house, waking everybody up. When everyone was out of their rooms and in the hall investigating, the fire alarms stopped. There was no fire or smoke. All the doors and windows were locked. There was no reason for the alarms to go off.

Since then, the fire alarms — plus the alarms on the doors and windows — would go off without reason. One time, they found the front door open. No one in the family admitted to coming downstairs and opening the door. Instead, they distinctly remembered closing and locking it. What was even stranger was that the alarm system was still set. Why did the alarm not go off that time? How could the alarm be set when it could only be armed when the door was closed?

The following day, the alarms went off again. Having had enough, the family called the company that installed the alarms and had the system replaced. When the same thing happened with the new alarms, they called the company again. A technician came immediately to examine the apparent glitch that was happening with the new set. With no obvious way of fixing it, the company instead replaced the new system with an upgraded one that utilized non-particle-based smoke detectors. Even with the upgrades, the alarms still went crazy.

Those were not the only strange things happening during that time. The family found one of their cats inside the boiler room a number of times. The problem was that there was no way the cat could get inside it because the doors were screwed in place. Their pets also started peeing on the counters — something they had never done before. They also became aggressive with each other and were often hissing at something unseen.

Unfortunately, the worst was yet to come.

One night, Ashley's sister was fast asleep when she was awakened by something beyond comprehension. It was around three thirty in the morning, and everyone else was sleeping. What woke her up was a voice. Someone whispered, "Hey!" in her ear. She could feel the other person's breath. Horrified, she quickly rolled off the bed and fell to the floor. She got up and turned the lights on. There was no one in the room. She checked the doors and windows. All of them were locked. Did she really hear and feel someone beside her, or had she imagined it?

Suddenly, a strange yet vaguely familiar odor emanated from somewhere. She went out to find the source. She followed the smell to the kitchen and found the stove burners were on. But there was no fire.

When their mother found out about that, she confronted Ashley. She realized that the strange events only started after Ashley came home. She asked her what really happened in Hawaii.

Ashley admitted that she hadn't really left her boyfriend. He had kicked her out. She said an old local woman cursed her while they were on a bus. Her boyfriend had been horrified. He didn't let Ashley back into their home that day until she agreed to have a relative determine if she was indeed cursed or not. The relative also performed a cleansing ritual on her.

Apparently, it didn't work.

Since being cursed, strange things started happening around Ashley. Bedroom doors were locked from the inside. Her ex-boyfriend suffered from nightmares. He even started to see and feel things—particularly a dark entity. The man, who was genuinely gentle and kind (he worked with disadvantaged children), started being abusive to her. He was scared, and he lashed out at her. He had no other option but to kick her out. Ashley ended up packing her things and moving back home. Much to her dismay, Ashley wasn't the only one who left Hawaii that day.

It turned out that Ashley was cursed by one of the local women in Waianae, Oahu where she had worked and stayed with her ex-boyfriend. The locals were jealous of her because she was a Caucasian girl dating a well-off, native Hawaiian man. The man was educated, had a good job, and was set to inherit a good fortune. Jealousy clouded the local women's opinions of her.

People threw insults at her, some even spat at her, and many told her to go back to where she had come from. Events became worse when an old lady, who was "sick of little white girls stealing all the native Hawaiian men," put a curse on her.

Were the problems that followed Ashley really because of a curse, or did a dark entity — a poltergeist, perhaps — fancy Ashley and follow her wherever she went? The answer remains unknown. Ashley continued to refuse help with the matter, even after she saw a ghost of a girl at the foot of her bed.

Obviously, Ashley had the unfortunate ability to see and attract the paranormal. Their mother gave Ashley an ultimatum: if she didn't get help, her mother would have no choice but to kick her daughter out. Stubborn as she was, Ashley moved out and got a place for herself.

Three days after Ashley left their home, the family was sitting in the living room with the door propped open by a full, five-gallon bucket of paint. Suddenly, the door slammed shut as if someone or something had furiously left the house.

Since then, the strange occurrences — the alarms, the misbehaving cats, etc. — stopped. Did the thing that haunted the house leave after Ashley did? Did it follow her? It seems so. Ashley has had four roommates since getting an apartment.

CHAPTER 9:

THE RENDLESHAM FOREST INCIDENT

Roswell isn't the only place famed and surrounded by accounts of unidentified flying objects and extraterrestrials. Another widely known incident took place in Suffolk, England, specifically in Rendlesham Forest, in the year 1980. It was late December when there were multiple reports of strange sightings.

Early in the morning of December 26th, 1980, a security staff member working in nearby Woodbridge reported seeing lights falling downward into Rendlesham Forest. At first, it was believed to be a downed aircraft; but when staff members accessed the forest to examine the possible crash site, what they saw was not something expected or familiar. They described the "craft" as being metallic, decked with multi-colored lights, glowing all over, and luminescent. As they drew closer to the anomaly, it seemed to move away, disappearing through the woods. Farm animals that happened to be in the area seemed especially agitated about the incident as well.

The police were dispatched to the area; but by the time they arrived, there were no traces of the strange scene that just occurred. The only lights that could be seen were from a lighthouse close by, which did not at all resemble the description of the odd lights the workers claimed to have seen. At this point, of course, it was still dark. When the investigation resumed after daylight, the workers discovered three strange impressions on the ground that together formed a triangle. They also saw burned debris from tree limbs. The police were called in once again. They thought it was possibly an animal of some kind that may have made the indentations on the ground. No possible explanation for the burned debris, however, was officially suggested. This is undoubtedly a strange occurrence, but it is the accumulation of multiple events here that lead to this area is sometimes referred to as "Britain's Roswell."

Shortly after the incident on December 26th, more investigations of the scene took place. A man and military commander by the name of Charles Halt entered the site, along with other workers, to test the area for radiation. They conducted tests in both areas, directly in the middle of the indentations made on the ground and the surrounding area. The instrument showed spikes in the "crash site" as well as random spikes up to about a half mile away. As Mr. Halt was making note of the radiation measurements, it was then that he and the other workers saw a flashing light that seemed to match the description of what was seen on the first night of the original incident.

In the year 2010, Mr. Charles Halt obtained a notarized affidavit. The document summarized the events that he had witnessed and the radiation results acquired from testing. It also contained his statement that he believed the incident to be of alien origin and that he suspected that both the UK and United States government worked together to cover up this extra-terrestrial activity. Mr. Halt served as a deputy and commander and is deemed reliable and credible. As such, his testimony serves as strong supporting evidence for believers of extraterrestrials.

CHAPTER 10:
MIRROR, MIRROR ON THE WALL

Amanda shared her tale of frequent visits to a friend's house in a rural farming area back in her younger years. They had sleepovers during which they would draw pictures and hang out. Whenever she would crash for the night, she would sleep on the couch in the living room. Near the couch was the television set. Two mirrors hung on the wall on either side of the TV.

During one of her sleepovers, she was walking by the TV when she noticed shadows moving behind her in the reflection of the screen. She dismissed it as a warp in the television and quickly forgot about it.

During another sleepover, she was in the living room again when she bent down to pick up her sketchbook. When she stood up, she was facing one of the mirrors. The reflection showed a man behind her.

The strange man was standing in the hallway which led to the living room. The man was medium-sized, older, and balding. She turned around, but no one was there. Horrified, she looked at the mirror once more but saw nothing behind her reflection. The old man was nowhere in sight.

The incident didn't stop her from sleeping over at her friend's house. Another night, she and her friend were hanging out on the couch when they suddenly heard the footsteps of a child running upstairs. There were no children in the house. Her friend had two adult siblings, but both of them were not at home at the time. Spooked, she skipped her routine of sleeping on the couch and decided to sleep in the bedroom with her friend instead.

But that didn't work.

In the middle of the night, she woke up and saw four of the posters taped to the wall getting peeled off. They weren't falling. The posters were slowly being peeled off by some invisible hand. Come morning, her friend brushed it aside and simply said that she needed better tape for her posters.

Eventually, her friend's family had to leave the place to stay in a cheaper home. After her friend moved out, she finally talked to her about the house and the weird events that she had experienced there. Her friend told her that she knew all along that her former home was haunted but didn't tell her so that she would still hang out with her. Her friend told her that the house used to belong to an old man who killed his granddaughter before committing suicide. Her friend then showed her a news article about the crime. The article had a picture of the old man. It was the same man she had seen in the mirror.

CHAPTER 11:
PILOT ENCOUNTERS WITH UFOS

With all the time they spend in the sky, plus their knowledge of aircraft, you can assume that among all people, pilots are perhaps the most likely to see unidentified flying objects. They are also most likely to be the ones to be able to identify various known types of aircraft. Due to their experience and knowledge, many people believe them to be extremely credible sources of information pertaining to unidentified flying objects and the possibility of extraterrestrials coming to Earth.

Just as recently as February of 2018, two pilots manning separate flights both reported strange, unidentified flying objects in the same location. Both airline pilots described seeing an odd, shiny object hovering over south Arizona. It was then investigated by the Federal Aviation Administration, but they were unable to explain or identify what had been seen.

In the afternoon of February 24th, 2018, the two pilots recounted the incident just after it unfolded, to the air traffic control center. It started with one of the pilots asking air traffic control whether or not another aircraft was passing above his location just 30 seconds prior. When the air traffic control center respondent replied with a resounding "no," the pilot then answered by telling them that something had definitely just passed over his plane. It had been flying quite high, several thousand feet above the jet manned by the pilot. Not having any explanation, air traffic control radioed another flight that was in a nearby area and asked this second pilot to keep a lookout for anything passing above it when it reached the desert area. Remarkably, just a few minutes later, the second pilot and his crew also saw something go past them, just as the first pilot had stated.

After several weeks of investigation, there are still no answers as to what it might have been. The Federal Aviation Administration was not able to confirm that any other aircraft of our own were anywhere nearby. They also do not believe it was a military craft or a meteorology-related device like a weather balloon. The Federal Aviation Administration is privy to all information regarding all forms of aircraft and flights, but they have no knowledge of anything that could possibly account for the unknown craft reported by the two pilots.

There are more than just pilot-stated accounts of unidentified flying objects. There are also videos that have gained popularity in the field. In 2015, US Navy pilots captured a video of their encounter with an unidentified flying object. One of the Navy pilots can be heard exclaiming, "What the [heck] is that thing?" The pilot then adds, "Wow, what is that, man?" The Department of Defense, however, declined to comment on the video and the event.

One of the most classic and long-standing pilot encounters with an unidentified flying object took place on October 1st in the year 1948. A fighter pilot for the North Dakota Air National Guard by the name of George Gorman had an encounter that lasted an astonishing 27 minutes. He was operating his assigned craft (a P-51 Mustang) in a flight across the country. While other pilots who were participating chose to land for that evening, Mr. Gorman decided to take advantage of the clear night sky and clock in some nighttime flying hours. When he was finally ready to land, he was informed by the control center that the only other aircraft near him was a "Piper Cub." He was able to see this craft himself, just a few hundred feet below his own. He then witnessed what appeared to him to be the tail lights of yet another craft passing beside him on the right side. However, this craft was not visible on the control center's radar system. Of course, George was curious and wanted to find out what the craft was; so, he made the decision to approach it and get a closer look. He reached within 1,000 yards from the strange object, close enough to describe it as being around 6 to 8 inches in diameter, translucent white in color, and alternately blinking on and off. He stated that when he got nearer to the object, the blinking then grew steady, and it pulled off sharply to the left.

Gorman was very perplexed. Curiosity got the best of him, and he decided to follow the object. After giving chase for quite a while and finally beginning to gain closer proximity, the strange flying object suddenly made a sharp turn and began flying directly towards his own plane. It nearly collided with Gorman but he made a downward dive. He then witnessed the object go over the top of his plane before it took yet another sharp turn, and headed straight at him once more. Again, it was just nearly about to collide with his plane when it suddenly jolted straight up at such a steep incline that Gorman's own plane stalled when he tried to trail after it. He did not see the strange object again after that point. When he made his report, he stated that he was engaged in this aerial game of chicken for 27 minutes before he finally landed his plane.

There were other interesting details included in Gorman's incident report as well. He stated that the object did not have an accompanying sound, nor did it appear to leave any trails of exhaust or smell of exhaust. He also reported that even when he reached a top speed of 400 miles per hour, he was still unable to keep up with the speed of whatever the strange object was. Additionally, he asserted that the object was being propelled with intelligent thought. Even though he pushed his own plane to its maximum capabilities, the unidentified object was able to go much faster, achieve much sharper and tighter turns, and ascend more rapidly and steeply.

Mr. Gorman was not the only person to encounter the strange, unidentified object that cloudless night. It was also seen by two air traffic control officers by the names of Lloyd Jensen and HE Johnson who were working at a nearby airport tower. Johnson reported seeing the previously mentioned Piper Cub, Gorman's plane, and the unidentified flying object. He stated that the unidentified flying object was traveling at a very high speed and appeared to be a perfectly round light, with no blurry edges or light rays leaving its form. The pilot of the Piper Cub also reported seeing the unidentified flying object, though he saw it both from his plane and after he had landed. He also described it as being very fast in speed. There were two other ground employees who reported witnessing the unidentified flying object as well. This is what adds not only to the unique quality of the event but also its credibility. It was witnessed by multiple parties from different vantage points, both in the air and on the ground. The object did not match the appearance of any known technology in existence, and its maneuvering abilities far surpassed our own.

CHAPTER 12:
SOMETHINGS IN THE ATTIC

Elizabeth and her roommate got a good scare while living in one of four apartments made out of an old Victorian house. Picture Victorian mansions in your head, and you'll instantly get haunting images of beautiful, old homes. Lots of stories have been told regarding such historic buildings. Many of those stories center around the lost souls or spirits of those who once lived in the houses long ago.

This particular Victorian home was no different. The place had undergone some upkeep, but the house maintained its style and haunting aura.

The women's apartment had a high ceiling and a laundry room, the same with the rest of the units. Theirs, however, had access to the attic. A three-foot-by-three-foot square was cut into the ceiling. Since the ceiling was really high, a ladder was needed to reach it. In order to climb up into the attic, the square in the ceiling had to be lifted in a way so that it was angled to avoid hitting the two beams placed there to keep the cover in place.

A couple of months had passed since they had moved into her new place when Elizabeth noticed that the access to the ceiling was open. The square was perched across the beams. She dismissed it, thinking it might have been open since they moved in and just hadn't been noticed at the time. The two of them had a hard time closing it since they didn't have a ladder. They tried standing on the washer, but they couldn't reach it. They even asked help from their tall neighbor, but the ceiling was still too high. In the end, the trio had to pile up boxes, one on top of another, until the six-foot-three-inches tall neighbor could reach the ceiling and close the access.

A few months later, the Elizabeth's roommate was alone in the apartment when she heard a loud noise. When she investigated, she saw the access was open once more. No one else was in their apartment, and there were no signs that someone had climbed up to open it.

Since then, they experienced other strange occurrences such as doors closing on their own, strange odors, and hearing footsteps. Perhaps the scariest of those incidents was the time the young woman was half-asleep on the couch and heard someone come in. Thinking it was her roommate coming home from work, she said hi without even opening her eyes. She heard footsteps walking through the living room and towards their room. As she heard the door to their room open, she opened her eyes just in time to see it shut. Curious as to why her roommate didn't say anything to her, she got up, knocked on the door, and opened it. There was no one there. Her roommate came home thirty minutes later.

CHAPTER 13:
BIZARRE ALIEN ABDUCTIONS

Alien abduction is considered the act of an extraterrestrial, non-human entity forcibly taking a human against his or her will, typically with the intent to study and experiment on our species. Many people have reported being abducted by extraterrestrials, detailing a range of different experiences. Some people wake up with just bits and pieces of strange memories and having lost several hours or more of their lives. Others awaken with vivid memories, and some are left with strange burns, markings, or bruises. Abduction is not a recent phenomenon, either. In fact, one of the most well-known, and perhaps the first, accounts of alien abduction took place in the year 1961.

Betty and Barney Hill

Two individuals by the names of Barney and Betty Hill were driving along in their vehicle one September night in 1961.

They were alone on the road and did not happen upon any other car or vehicle of any kind for quite some time. They did, however, see a strange light up in the sky that appeared to be following them. When they reached their destination, they felt very strange and oddly dirty. Their watches were no longer working, Betty's dress was inexplicably torn, and Barney's shoes were mysteriously scratched up. More shocking was the two hours of their journey that neither of them could recall.

They both decided to see a psychiatrist. After some sessions, some frightening memories of theirs regarding that night were uncovered. They recalled gray creatures that walked them aboard a disc-like structure that was described by Betty to be larger than her house. Once they were aboard, they were examined by the beings that then erased their memories and returned them to their car. By this time, two hours had passed and the couple was roughly 35 miles down the road from where they had been. Their recovered memories about the experience launched an Air Force investigation as part of the secret government initiative dedicated to investigating unidentified flying objects and possible interactions with extraterrestrials. Their experience was also the first well-publicized account of alien abduction.

Allagash

This incident took place in the year 1976. Four individuals had decided to go camping in a wooded, isolated area in Maine. They spent an enjoyable first night camping; but on the second night, things took a turn for the strange. At first, the campers noticed a bright light but nothing else of concern accompanied it. They then decided to give night fishing a try. While on their canoe, they saw the bright light once again. In an effort to figure out what it might be, one of them used a flashlight to signal an SOS at the light, to see if it would respond in some way. The light then began to grow and expand until it had enveloped all four people. This is the last thing any of them can recall before they woke up back at their camping space. They could not remember anything that happened after the light encased them, including how they got back to land from their canoe. A significant amount of time seemed to have elapsed, as the fire they had built before setting out to fish, which they intended to last for quite a while, was just mere embers.

After returning from the trip, one of the men began to experience strange nightmares. He dreamed of weird beings that had large heads and long necks, big luminescent eyes, and no eyelids. Their hands appeared insect-like and only had four large fingers. The other three individuals also began experiencing dreams of the very same nature with similar details.

In the year 1988, one of the individuals decided to attend an unidentified flying object conference. The conference host listened to his account of the strange experience and recommended that he and the others attempt regressive hypnosis. All of the individuals underwent this form of therapy and uncovered disturbing memories of being abducted by alien beings as well as being examined by them, which included obtaining bodily fluid samples and tissue specimen. All four of them were consistent in recounting and describing the beings in the same way. They were able to sketch pictures of the examination equipment used, and their depictions of the beings were eerily similar as well. All of them were also further evaluated and determined to be mentally sound; additionally, they all passed a polygraph (lie detector) test when questioned about the event.

Elizabeth "Liz" Klarer

Liz was a very interesting woman even before her claimed alien abduction. She studied music, aviation, and meteorology. She served the Royal Air Force as well as the British Military Intelligence. In the year 1956, Liz was on a hill named, strangely enough, "Flying Saucer Hill", where she claimed to have been abducted by extraterrestrials. She maintains that the alien species referred to themselves as the "Alpha Centauri System" and hailed from the planet "Meton." She recounts meeting a male of the species by the name of "Akon," and says that the two of them fell in love. After a brief courtship, Liz claims she became pregnant and soon gave birth to a crossbred child. The child was taken back to the aliens' home planet of Meton, so that it could be taught about the galaxy.

Linda Napolitano

A Manhattan native by the name of Linda Napolitano claims she was abducted via her apartment bedroom window in the year 1989. She recounts being taken aboard an extraterrestrial ship by "grays" and then being put through a series of invasive experimentations. After her encounter, she initially did not have much memory of the incident. Every once in a while, a fragment of memory about the abduction would return; but even then, she could only recall being forcibly taken and being placed in a room for examination. No other details surfaced; that is, until she decided to undergo hypnosis therapy. By recovering lost memories via therapy, as well as giving time for her mind to heal from the trauma on its own, the details of the event began to surface and come together. Additional credibility was given to Linda's encounter when two men came forth, claiming to have witnessed her abduction. They had no contact with Linda, yet their testimonies perfectly aligned with the recovered details of hers.

Pascagoula River

In the year 1973, two individuals were fishing at the Pascagoula River, when they suddenly heard a strange, unfamiliar low buzzing noise accompanied by bright flashing blue-hued lights. A strange craft appeared, and the two men were forcibly taken aboard by what they described as 3 human-like alien creatures. An examination of the men ensued, and after roughly 20 minutes, they were returned via levitation to the ground on the pier where they had been fishing.

The men immediately went to the authorities to report the incident. When the officers left the interrogation room where the men were being questioned, their conversation was recorded, unbeknownst to them. Here is a paraphrased version of the conversation:

Man 1: I've never seen anything like that before, never in my life. We can't force anyone to believe...

(Man 2 interrupts)

Man 2: I don't want to just sit here anymore, we should see a doctor.

Man 1: They have to listen to us; they need to believe us.

Man 2: Did you see the door? How it just came up like that?

Man 1: Yeah, I have no idea, no idea how it opened.

Man 2: It just... was there... and then they appeared, just like that.

Man 1: I know... it sounds unbelievable... we can't make them believe it...

Man 2: I was paralyzed, I couldn't even move...

Man 1: They're not going to believe us until it's too late. I knew there were other worlds... but I never thought this would happen to me.

Donna and Clayton

A couple, husband Clayton and wife Donna, claim that they have been abducted multiple times. Clayton even says he suspects that extraterrestrials have been observing him throughout his entire life. These memories of abductions resurface during therapy sessions. Their therapist, strangely enough, says he did not believe in alien life or UFOs.

Both Donna and Clayton have drawn pictures of what they claim to be the extraterrestrials they encountered. They have also recounted their stories for different media platforms multiple times as well. One particularly alarming claim was that an unborn fetus was forcibly taken from Donna by one of the extraterrestrials.

Amy

A young woman named Amy claims she was abducted through her living room window by some kind of unidentified flying object. According to Amy, she was not the only person who was in on the experience, as the incident also involved her husband and a friend of hers, Petra.

It was night time. Amy's husband had already gone to bed and retired for the night. Amy was relaxing in the living room while Petra was doing some late-night reading in a separate room. Suddenly, Petra was disturbed by an extremely bright light and the sound of breaking glass. Petra says she witnessed a stream of light pulling Amy out through the broken window in the living room. Amy appeared to be asleep as she was being lifted away.

Amy's husband was awakened, and both he and Petra searched the entirety of the house and the immediate area. When they still could not locate Amy, they decided to call the police. Amy reappeared after a while, many miles away from her home. She had strange unexplained marks on the inside areas of her thighs. There was an unusual amount of body hair that had not been there previouly—as if a considerable amount of time had passed.

Jesse Long

A man by the name of Jesse Long has claimed he has been abducted by alien beings numerous times. The abductions started all the way back in 1957 when he was still a young boy at the age of 5, in Tennessee. Jesse had been playing with his brother in a wooded area; and this is where they discovered a strange, round structure. He recounts that a tall figure then appeared, and he saw a bright flash. At this time, he and his brother were frozen, unable to speak or move. He states that he was taken aboard a craft and placed on a cold, metallic table, where multiple tall figures poked him around and examined his legs.

Over the course of the next several years, Jesse says he was abducted by these tall beings repeatedly for experimentation. One incident involved extracting the sperm that he claimed was then used for interbreeding with one of the female alien beings. In the year 1990, he says the beings returned and showed him an infant that was supposedly his crossbred child. Over an additional period of time, he declares that he has met 9 more crossbred alien-human children resulting from their experimentations on him. There is no way to either confirm or deny his statements. Jesse himself has acknowledged that his claims sound outlandish. Nevertheless, he insists that the stories he has told about his experiences are completely true.

Robert Taylor

Robert Taylor was a woodsman in Livingston, Scotland in the year 1979. He was on his way to the woods where he was to work that day, when he suddenly came across an unidentified flying object in a clearing. Two small circular orbs moved simultaneously from the object. They made a sound as they came towards him, stopping by his side and seizing him by his clothing. They proceeded to forcefully drag him to the unidentified flying object that had landed in the field. On closer observation, the orbs appeared to be smaller versions of the UFO. His senses were then bombarded with a horrible, sickening smell before he blacked out and lost consciousness.

When he awoke, the orbs and the unidentified flying object had vanished. His dog was still there with him, though it was acting scared, running around and barking loudly. When Robert tried to call to his dog to calm him down, he discovered he had no voice. He also felt very feeble and was too weak to stand. He spent some time crawling along on the ground before he finally gained enough strength to stand upright. He slowly made his way back to his vehicle, where he planned to use the two-way radio. However, he still did not regain his voice. He began driving his vehicle towards home but soon became stuck in some mud. He had no choice then but to take the one-mile walk to his home. When he got there, his wife saw that he looked quite terrible and was visibly shaken. She called the police, who then launched an investigation but were unable to identify the strange tracks left in the area. There were also no aircraft scheduled to be operating in the area at the time of the incident.

Travis Walton

Travis Walton was a woodsman as well, working with a team in Snowflake, Arizona. He and his group were making the return trip home one night when they suddenly witnessed an extremely bright light. Worried that a plane may have crashed, they drove towards it. What they found was not at all familiar, and did not bear resemblance to an airplane. Travis got out of his truck and approached the craft. As he came closer, a beam of bright light quickly shone out from the craft and pulled Travis in. His crewmates were terrified and fled the scene to call for help.

One member of the group contacted the police and spoke to Sheriff Ellison. At first, he merely reported that a member of their work crew had gone missing and made no mention of additional details. But when the sheriff met the group for questioning, they gave a full account of the incident. Sheriff Ellison noted that they were all visibly upset, and some were even tearful. It seemed to be a genuine emotional response.

Officers were dispatched to the area in question but there was no evidence to support their claim of a UFO. Police began to grow suspicious of the group, speculating that they had concocted a tale to cover up the murder of Travis. The men were then made to undergo rigorous interrogation and lie detector tests; after which, their story was still found to be consistent and sound. At this point, 5 days had passed with no leads on finding Travis Walton. Then, he suddenly resurfaced. He was disoriented and confused, thinking that he had only been gone for a few short hours when, in fact, it had been days. He said he had been taken aboard the craft, met and questioned by three, bald beings with large eyes, as well as other creatures that performed a variety of experiments on him. His account of the abduction was consistent with those of his fellow group members.

Carol and Helen Thomas

On March 30th in the year 1988, Carol and her daughter, Helen, set out for work at a nearby mill. They took the same roads, paths, and alleyways as they usually do. Walking along, they suddenly heard an unfamiliar, low-frequency humming sound. This was not something they had ever heard before, let alone on their trip to work. The strange sound seemed to be coming from above them. Suddenly an extremely bright light appeared, rendering them unable to see. As the light eventually began to fade, both women started to regain their normal frame of mind, though feeling sick and dizzy. Even when their minds remained feeling a bit foggy and they were not feeling so well, they continued on their way to work. When they arrived, a security staff member informed them that they were, in fact, already several hours late. The incident felt like short moments to them; but somehow, they were missing several hours of time, for which they could not account.

Over the course of the next few days, both women began to suffer from more than just feeling a bit sick. Their skin broke out, and a strange rash and blisters appeared. Their mental state also began to suffer, as they were riddled with intense feelings of anxiety. They didn't seek any psychological help immediately; but after a few years, they recounted their experience to a UFO expert by the name of Tony Todd, who questioned them while under the influence of hypnosis. Both of the women uncovered memories of being taken into a brightly-lit room and placed on an examination table. They described an unusual netting that was used to restrain their legs with what they said felt like weight to hold them down. They said that strange alien beings with large eyes and large heads performed a variety of tests and experiments on them, including inserting a tube into their abdomens and removing eggs. The women described the creatures further, stating that everything was wet, as if they were exuding some kind of liquid. One of the creatures was particularly fascinated with Helen's coat, thoroughly examining and caressing the material, which resulted in it becoming soaked with whatever liquid was coating everything.

Garry Wood

On the night of August 17th in the year 1992, Garry Wood and his friend, Colin, were driving along A70 when they suddenly witnessed a strange, black object nearby. They both watched as the strange object drew closer, and then suddenly produced a bright white wall of light in front of them and their vehicle. Garry, who was driving, did not stop, as he was mesmerized by the strange light. He continued to drive. Abruptly, their trance was broken and the car was no longer moving forward. In fact, it had not only come to a complete stop but was somehow facing the opposite direction. Neither of the men recalled turning the car around. Checking his watch, Garry realized they had lost about an hour. The men felt sure that something was truly wrong.

Both men underwent therapy to unveil memories regarding their experience and the lost time. What they discovered was quite terrifying. Both of them uncovered memories of being painfully electrocuted as they had driven into the wall of light. They then recounted being taken by three alien beings aboard a craft that was on the road. Their clothing was taken off and they were examined, all the while hearing blood-curdling human screams around them. The examination appeared to be overseen by another creature that they described as being tall, with a large head and large eyes. Garry recalled this fourth creature communicating with him via telepathy, telling him that they were already there, and "we are coming here."

John Day

John Day was a family man, who had no existing belief in UFOs or extraterrestrials; that is, until one day in Essex in the year 1974. John, his wife, and their children were driving home one night, a trip that usually took about 30 minutes. This meant that they would be home just before 10 PM. When they arrived, they set about their usual routine of getting the kids ready for bed, during which John checked the time. It was nearly 1 AM, not just before 10 PM, as he had previously thought. Oddly, their trip had taken more than 3 hours.

Over the course of the next few days, everyone in the family began having disturbing nightmares. These dreams were so terrifying that they feared to fall asleep. Both parents were also suffering from feelings of mental confusion and anxiety. A local UFO research group suggested to John that they should undergo hypnosis in an effort to recover memories from their lost hours. John did as suggested. While under hypnosis, he recalled traveling into a strange mist that appeared to be made of light which had come down from the sky. Another more focused light then appeared; and the vehicle, with the entire family inside, was lifted and transported to what John described as an alien "spaceship."

John's memories were pretty fuzzy even during hypnosis therapy. He could recall a strange metallic arm moving above him, as well as feelings of being pricked by something multiple times. The only detail he could recall about the interior of the craft was there were no "seams"—the furnishings were built seamlessly into the walls. He simply remembered coming to in their car, in the driveway of their home.

"Sharon"

Sharon lived in Yorkshire, a mother of two children. One afternoon, she was listening to the radio, when the program began airing the accounts of people who claimed to have been abducted by extraterrestrials. This piqued Sharon's interest, leading her to get additional information. For quite a while, she had been having very strange, unexplainable experiences. She suffered from missing time, and would suddenly have inexplicable markings on her body. She had strange feelings of anxiety, but could not point to any cause. Thus, she reached out for help.

She agreed to undergo hypnosis therapy, during which time she uncovered lost memories. She recounted being taken aboard an extraterrestrial craft and being subjected to painful experimentation. She also remembered that she was not the only person there. In fact, she recalled being rounded up with several other people as if they were waiting to be transported elsewhere like cattle. She even seemed to recognize one man, whom she identified as "Nigel." Still, one rediscovered memory really stood out from the rest.

Sharon recalled walking to the end of a garden at her family home to have a cigarette when she was just a teenager. Suddenly, she was lifted up and taken aboard an extraterrestrial craft. She said there was a strange form of writing on the wall, which she described as Egyptian. She was examined, and then was told that humankind needed to care for the planet and stop polluting it. She then recalled being instructed to learn about "the pyramids," and heard "we put [them] here!"

The Deverows

It was just after 5 PM on a January day in North Yorkshire in the year 2005, as the Deverow family traveled along the A65 road. Anne, her daughter Rachel, and Rachel's two children were all present. Suddenly they saw a strange bright light that appeared to be following them. They continued to observe the light as it trailed along for several minutes before it leaped closer and then suddenly accelerated away, out of sight.

They continued on their trip, which was just a 10-minute drive, when they realized an hour had passed. Without anyone noticing, it was now past 6 PM. Confusion set in, as no one was able to account for the lost hour. They tried to move on and not think about the incident. However, one of the children began having very strange dreams, in which he said he was "flying" over fields inside of a bubble.

After some time, Rachel agreed to try hypnotherapy to try to uncover what had happened during their lost hour. She recalled that at the time of the incident, the light seemed to levitate her and her family up into a strange craft. She described the interior of the craft as not being like an "inside" at all. Rather, it looked as if they were in a vast, deep space. She also described a bright light above them and many other smaller lights darting around, examining them. The family reports that they have continued seeing strange lights over their house since the incident.

Antonio Vilas-Boas

The night of October 26th in the year 1957 was a typical evening as Antonio tended to his farm. Suddenly, a strange, extremely bright light appeared in the sky right above him. It continued to move at a high speed across the fields, and abruptly stopped. As Antonio observed, stunned, he realized that it was a strange craft; and it was landing right in his field. Antonio recounts that three creatures wearing some kind of space suit exited from the craft and forcibly dragged him aboard, where he was taken to what he described as a metal room.

In this room appeared an attractive human-esque female with what Antonio recounted as having "platinum blond" hair. He narrated that she seemed to want to seduce him as he sat there, confused. What went through Antonio's mind?

It is not certain, but he admits that he had intercourse with the female entity not only once, but twice. He believes that the sole purpose of the abduction was to create a crossbred species, which he obliged.

Gustavo "Gus" Gonzalez

One night in the year 1954 in Petare, Venezuela, Gus and his friend were taking a trip to a meat wholesaler to purchase pork. Suddenly, the road on which they were traveling on was blocked by a weird luminescent orb. Gus recounts that three hairy-looking creatures exited the orb and came towards them. A struggle then ensued.

Gus says that one of the creatures jumped on the back of his friend in an attempt to subdue him while Gus was impaired by a strange bright light. Scared for their lives, Gus was able to retrieve his pocket knife and attempted to fight creatures off; but the knife didn't appear to even scratch their strange, thick skins. After struggling for some time, the creatures then began to retreat back to their craft and quickly took off. This story sounds pretty bizarre and far-fetched, but Gus maintains it is a true account of their extraterrestrial encounter.

A study performed 30 years after the "Betty and Barney Hill" incident report estimates that over one million people believe that they had been abducted by extraterrestrials. An explanation often offered by skeptics is that these individuals are simply suffering from a distorted sense of reality. They have misinterpreted information surrounding an event, which then leads them to this far-fetched belief. However, additional studies on individuals with these experiences indicate that they were psychologically healthy and had no history of any other mental disturbances.

Another explanation for extraterrestrial abduction is neuropsychological disorders. No, this is not a type of mental illness. Rather, it deals with issues like sleep paralysis. Simply put, the strange phenomena known as sleep paralysis is caused by a malfunction in the brain wherein part of the conscious mind wakes up, but the state of paralysis used to protect the body during sleep is still intact. During this time, the brain is experiencing aspects of both being awake and being asleep, which distorts and misinterprets reality. Still, people who claim to have been abducted insist that they were never asleep in order for this to be the case. Why would they be, when some of these events took place while they were driving or working?

Alien abductions: are they real or just symptoms of a combination of mental disturbance and mass hysteria? There is an overwhelming lack of tangible, scientific evidence; thus, this phenomenon is often dismissed as false memories, suggestibility, or resulting from different types of psychological disturbances. The number of reported abductions and their similarities, however, are enough to convince some people of the legitimacy of these encounters. Moreover, the people that come forth with their abduction stories often face ridicule; so they neither seek publicity or media attention, nor do they receive compensation of any kind. This poses the question: if there is no obvious "reward" of these "tall tales," why would anyone bother with them? This is often the logic that eliminates the possibility of people falsifying reports for monetary gain or public attention and media coverage.

While believers point out the consistencies of the different accounts from individuals who have never had contact with each another, skeptics point to variances in accounts that seem to exist from culture to culture in different parts of the world. Skeptics also draw lines connecting the stories of people's abductions to the details and storylines of science fiction movies and TV shows like *The X-Files* and *Invaders from Mars*. Regression hypnosis therapy is also largely discredited, as there have been many cases in which the therapist administering the therapy was actually implanting false memories into the patient, in order to either prove their own theories or gain media attention in their field. Still, thousands of people all over the world are firm believers in extraterrestrials, citing Paleolithic cave drawings that depict flying craft and strange alien-looking creatures.

Whether you are a concrete disbeliever or a skeptic, consider this: there are an unknown number of solar systems, planets, and thus, other worlds entirely. If life can exist here, is there not a high probability that other forms of life - perhaps varieties that we cannot even fathom - exist elsewhere? The universe is vast; so are the chances of extraterrestrial life.

CHAPTER 14:

DADDY'S HERE

This is the story of a registered nurse who worked the late shift. It was shared by her husband Dan.

The nurse, who typically worked in the cardiac ward, was helping out and volunteered in the Alzheimer's unit. When doing her rounds, she normally saved a specific patient for last. All the nurses disliked the elderly woman because she was miserably mean to everyone.

One night, the nurse finally finished catering to all of her other patients and was on her way to the elderly woman's room. The respiratory therapist arrived at her door the same time as the nurse. The two of them decided to do their tasks together. When the two of them entered the room, the patient was hysterical. The woman was screaming and jumping on the bed. Worst of all, the walls of the bathroom were smeared with defecation. The two medical personnel first dealt with the old lady and eventually calmed her down. After that was taken care of, the two were able to return to their scheduled duties—which by that point included cleaning up the bathroom.

After about three hours, they left the room and placed a "Do Not Disturb" sign on the door so the elderly patient could sleep. They were still at the patient's door, standing on opposite sides and complaining about what just happened when they noticed a huge man walking down the hallway of the hospital. He was wearing a red, plaid shirt, overalls, working boots, and a John Deere baseball cap. His overall appearance reminded them of a farmer. The man, obviously annoyed, walked past the two and straight into the room. He even slammed the door after him!

Shocked, the nurse immediately went inside with the therapist right behind her. They were stunned to see that the man wasn't in there. They looked everywhere. They checked under the bed. Nothing. The nurse went inside the bathroom. It was empty. They checked the curtains. Still no sign of the strange man. The windows were shut. It was impossible for the man to have jumped out the window and close it in time for the two not to see him.

That was when they noticed the elderly woman was awake and sitting up in bed. She was staring into space. The nurse asked the old woman if she had seen a person come inside her room. To their astonishment, the patient said, "Yes."

"It was my daddy," the elderly woman continued. "He came to take me home tonight so that you mean people won't be able to hurt me anymore."

"That's great," the nurse responded. "Now how about you get some rest before he comes to pick you up." The old woman obliged and went back to bed without fighting them.

The elderly patient passed away that very night.

CHAPTER 15:
THE MORE RECENT DEVELOPMENTS

Taking what could be considered a detour, we will explore some of the more contemporary encounters and sightings in this chapter. The modern times are particularly interesting when it comes to the UFO phenomenon for a couple of reasons. First, the technological advancements that we have seen since the 2000s have made it much easier for the average person to document any strange occurrences. Secondly, the number of sighting reported has grown due to this reason.

Of course, other technological breakthroughs have made it that much easier for fakes and hoaxes, which is why we should be careful and skeptical when examining any new reports. With that in mind, we will investigate some rather compelling developments in the UFO sphere.

The Pentagon UFO Investigation Program Footage

Not often does a major development in this matter come from the Pentagon. In fact, we all know that the Pentagon is one of the usual suspects when it comes to cover-ups and theories of a government conspiracy to suppress the truth about the phenomenon. Nonetheless, December of 2017 brought about what many UFO enthusiasts and investigators consider to be a giant leap on the path toward the truth about alien life forms and their visitations to Earth.

It was in December when it was revealed to the New York Times, among other outlets, that the US Department of Defense had been running a secretive program called the Advanced Aviation Threat Identification Program between 2007 and 2012. The objective of this effort, officials stated, was to investigate UFO incidents involving military personnel. The program has since been discontinued according to the Pentagon, but data is most likely still being collected. Many of the incidents have been well-documented and even filmed or photographed.

Considering these revelations, one incident seized the spotlight and caught the eye of the public. The encounter itself occurred in the afternoon hours of November 14, 2004, and it primarily involved two F/A-18 fighter jets belonging to the US Navy, taking off from a Nimitz class aircraft carrier.

Pilots David Fravor and Jim Slaight were in the air as part of a training mission, some one-hundred miles off the coast of California. The events were set in motion when they were contacted by a nearby Navy cruiser.

As the story was told by Fravor, it turned out that the vessel, USS Princeton, was in the area investigating unidentified craft for some two weeks prior. The bizarre crafts were observed making impossible, erratic maneuvers, which involved seizing great altitude at incredible speeds, dropping back down, hovering, and disappearing from the Navy's radars. The pilots were thus called in to investigate an anomaly that was tracked in the area at that very time.

The jets arrived on the scene soon after but couldn't identify anything out of the ordinary at first, neither by visual contact nor on their radars. Then, Fravor reported, they noticed a disturbance in the water and what appeared to be an object just under the ocean's surface. Some fifty feet above the churning anomaly, they spotted a flying object that measured roughly forty feet in length and had the shape of a Tic Tac. The UFO was making random, erratic motions, but it didn't seem to go anywhere.

When Fravor attempted to approach the craft to get a better look, it whooshed away at an unprecedented speed, the likes of which he had never seen in his entire career. He reported that he was unsettled by what he had seen. In response, the pilots-maintained communication with the cruiser and set up a rallying point sixty miles further. As they set off on their way, the radar operators on the cruiser reported picking up a signature again – the UFO was already at their rally point. When they finally caught up and arrived on location, the craft was nowhere to be found.

The story of these pilots and their clear acknowledgment of the incredible capabilities of these crafts are fascinating enough, but the real kicker is the footage that was recorded by both of their planes. This footage is now available for everyone to view in its unaltered form throughout the Internet. One of the objects is clearly shown as it was being tracked by the gun camera in all its incredible mystique. Indeed, the shape of the object does resemble a giant Tic Tac as it flies through the clouds and glows on the gun camera. More shocking is the craft's maneuvers, though, which seem impossible. The craft was able to rotate and adjust itself with utmost ease all while moving at great speeds. The footage also contains the original audio recording of the communication between the two pilots as they are trying to make sense of the UFO they are following. They have little success, however, and it's clear from their exchange that they are both bewildered.

The pilots never discussed their supernatural encounter until last December's revelation of the program. As incredible as the story and the footage are, it's unsettling to think that it's most likely just the tip of the iceberg, as we have no way of knowing what else the military could be keeping in its vaults.

UFO Causes Airport to Shut Down

This incident transpired in Hangzhou, China, back in 2010 amid a wave of similar sightings in the country at that time. It remains a largely unexplained mystery with quite a few theories as to what may have been at play, but its impact is a well-documented fact.

The strange event began on July 7 at around 8:40 PM, the crewmembers of a plane that was incoming to the Xiaoshan Airport reported to traffic control that they've spotted an unidentified craft in their proximity. Traffic control reacted with caution by proceeding to ground all scheduled flights leaving the airport, as well as directing incoming ones to other airports. The shutdown lasted for about an hour until the object disappeared, disrupting eighteen flights in total.

The Chinese media and the public quickly caught wind of the incident, and numerous photos and sighting reports started coming in, describing and showing a mysterious, elongated, glowing object in the night sky.

One witness described that he noticed a powerful light beam overhead while taking a leisurely stroll that evening. He immediately got out his camera and took a photo that was later publicized, clearly showing a brightly lit object just under the clouds. Like many of the other witnesses, though, he was unable to confirm whether the object he photographed was the one that was spotted by the flight crew, causing the airport to shut down.

An official investigation into the phenomenon was launched soon thereafter by the authorities, and although one would expect the opposite, things started to get increasingly quiet after that. China Daily, a Chinese news outlet, alleged that an anonymous source confirmed a day later that the investigators successfully solved the case. However, the authorities decided to withhold the findings due to what they described as a "military connection" to the incident. Of course, that meant the Chinese military, but many of the witnesses and theories were skeptical, suggesting that the object was either extraterrestrial or belonging to a foreign military organization. Either way, the speculations were only fueled further by the fact that there were numerous other sightings over the week before the incidents.

The authorities went on to confirm that the object seen in the photo was confirmed not to be the one that disrupted the airport, and the matter was then dropped as far as the public was concerned.

2015 California Sighting

This was yet another strange occurrence that the authorities described as being connected to the military and having nothing to do with extraterrestrials. Early in November of 2015, residents in Los Angeles, San Diego, and some other places in Arizona and Nevada reported and filmed a huge, blue light leaving a trail as it blazed across the night sky, resembling a comet of sorts.

The weird event was witnessed by thousands of people and footage of it is abundant. Speculations immediately ran wild and, folks from all walks of life took to the Internet to voice their theories, which ranged from extraterrestrials to meteors. Though it was somewhat delayed, the military did come out to comment on the incident, saying that it was nothing, but an unarmed Trident missile test undertaken by a US Navy submarine. No further comments were issued by the authorities and, based on their take on the situation, no investigation was necessary, leaving the matter at that.

Although there was no compelling evidence to suggest that this was disinformation, many people were less than satisfied with the explanation. Some witnesses also reported seeing several UFOs, not just the one that was sighted by most. Considering how strikingly prominent and noticeable the glaring light show in the sky was, it was certainly somewhat strange that the Navy didn't inform the public of an upcoming test beforehand. Apart from theories concerning extraterrestrials on social media, many emergency calls were made by the concerned public as the events unfolded. This turn of events or even a greater panic was to be expected by authorities, which really begs the question of why the test remained unannounced. The delay in the military's acknowledgment of the incident was also quite peculiar.

Just one day later, the incident took another turn that may or may not have been related. Not far from where the strange light was seen, in San Jose, a local woman reported a strange incident not long before midnight. She claimed to have heard an unsettling shriek come from her yard. When she went to investigate, she found the corpse of a bizarre, terrifying creature lying in the grass. She took a photograph and posted it online, fueling further speculation and yielding a few other explanations from users. While the creature looked like it could be a malformed animal fetus or a miscarriage of some kind, its true nature remains unconfirmed.

Mexico City UFO Mothership Videos

Mexico City has been the location of numerous UFO encounters and sightings in the past, and this is an ongoing trend in the current era. A particularly shocking and compelling incident took place on May 22, 2009.

Strangely enough, this event didn't receive much coverage and discussion, so no known, official attempts were made to explain what had transpired on that day, but the footage, including two videos, is more than enough to get one's mind racing. It is well that the footage is so convincing and apparently genuine because there isn't a whole lot of information about the case.

What we do know is the time when the sightings occurred and the names of the two individuals who recorded and released the footage to a Mexican TV station, where it was first aired. The locals, Pedro Hernandez and Alfredo Carrillo, shot their videos a few miles apart, thus giving us two angles of view on the phenomenon. One video shows the object(s) illuminated by the sun while the other captured their underside that was shadowed.

What can be clearly seen on both videos truly boggles the mind. There appears to be one larger object moving across the sky and shooting out swarms of much smaller craft that resemble flocks of UAVs or drones. While the smaller objects appear as though they are just floating dead in the air as they are gushing out of the main object apparently by force, they soon assume control over themselves. In fact, the deliberate and seemingly intelligent nature of their movements quickly takes on quite an eerie appearance. Not only are the objects moving on their own, but they are making quick, erratic, unnatural maneuvers around their perceived mothership and further from it.

What's also shocking is the sheer number of these smaller aircrafts in comparison to the main vessel's size. It would appear impossible that the primary UFO could contain that many independent, smaller UFOs inside of it, but that is precisely what's happening in the footage. As you may or may not know, there has been talk for a while now about various military technologies that are being developed and could possibly resemble the phenomenon that the men witnessed. Swarms of drones are not the realm of science fiction anymore, but the maneuvers that the craft in the footage are making and the lack of official comment on the matter leave a lot of room for interpretation.

Of course, the footage has been available all over the Internet for quite a while now, so everyone who is curious can and should inspect the videos for themselves and try to draw their own conclusion as to what they are seeing. To most, the objects are bound to come across as very unnatural indeed.

Cigar-Shaped Lightshow over Paris

Another unexplained sighting that was followed by very unsettling video footage happened quite recently in April of 2017, allegedly in the night skies of the Parisian suburbs.

A major YouTube channel, "Secureteam10," which revolves around publishing various UFO evidence received the video in question at that time from an unknown individual claiming to have filmed it in the proximity of the French capital. The channel hosts found the video to be fascinating and decided to publish it while maintaining a dose of skepticism and making it clear that the source is unknown. The email through which the footage was received was also presented and shown to be genuine.

The footage itself is quite straightforward and of decent quality, showing one glowing, cigar-shaped object hovering in the distance and radiating a powerful, flickering beam of light at a downward angle. Around the main object were multiple other lights, some of which also just hovered while others seemed to move back and forth, disappear, and then come back into the frame.

The main object in the video showed a striking similarity to the UFO that was photographed in China back in 2010, having a very similar shape and shining a potent light from the sky. This time, however, no investigative efforts were reported to have taken place, and the incident remains largely a mystery, particularly due to the lack of information provided by the sender, who is yet to reappear since submitting his or her findings.

As always, various explanations were brought forward by the many viewers of the footage, but none of them could be proven beyond a reasonable doubt, of course. Another incident that was compared to this one was a 2014 sighting on the Gold Coast, Australia, which has been quite a hotspot for UFO activity over the years.

These have been some of the more contemporary developments and incidents that were noticed and emphasized by UFO enthusiasts and regular folks alike. While any mysterious event in the sky is always exciting and fascinating, everyone should remember to maintain a dose of healthy skepticism when sources are unconfirmed. Officially confirmed cases are an entirely different story, though, and instances such as that of the US Navy pilots are truly unsettling or exciting, depending on your perspective.

It also begs one to wonder, if there were enough UFO encounters to drive the military to allocate some $22 million from its budget to investigate the phenomenon, and if they only released a handful of videos from a five-year program, what else could they have? All we can do is hope that more evidence sees the light of day and keep digging for the truth, the bits of which at least are bound to crop up every now and then.

Let us now go back to exploring a couple more prominent cases, regardless of their time, because the testimonies and evidence are nowhere near depleted.

CHAPTER 16:

WHO'S IN THE WATER

Adam relates a story that happened to him back in 1971. He was in his late 20s and staying at his folks' place in Rose Hill, Mauritius. His father came home one day with a South African couple tagging along. The two were tourists, and his dad invited them to stay at their place for a few days.

To accommodate the guests, the family organized a weekend camping trip in Flic en Flac on the west coast. When Saturday came, the group proceeded to Flic en Flac and set up camp. The family and their guests spent the day catching fish and crabs, swimming, and feasting on barbecue.

At around nine in the evening, the group was huddled by the campfire and staring at the stars. Suddenly, a strange noise ripped through the air. It sounded like a woman wailing. At first, they thought that it must have been some kind of animal. The sound came and went for some time, increasing their unease.

In the darkness, a figure mysteriously appeared in the water about thirty or forty meters away from them. It was a woman with long, black hair dressed in a flowing, white dress. She was walking from the sea to the beach. Once the woman got to the beach, she kept walking until she vanished into the trees.

Everyone saw her but couldn't explain what had happened. Adam finally got up to check on the woman. After a bit, he walked back to the group, slightly unnerved. He told them that he hadn't seen anything out there: No houses, no lights, no woman.

They all sat in silence. Their senses were on full alert. Suddenly, they heard flapping sounds from a nearby tree. Birds or bats were flying away as if someone or something had disturbed their slumber. The group sat still in fear. The feeling that something was wrong tingled against their spines. In the eeriness of the night, they couldn't shake the sense that they were being watched.

The South African couple started looking around when something heavy fell in front of the group. Adam stood up to see what it was. Again, there was nothing. The rest of the group stood up and joined the search, but they all came up empty handed. Worry wormed its way through their stomachs. They wondered if they should stay and sleep the rest of the night, or if they should just leave?

They were trying to decide what to do when a piercing scream filled the air. It was as if a woman was being attacked somewhere near them. The group instinctively packed up their things. Coconuts started falling and rolling towards them like they were being deliberately thrown. The fear in the air was almost tangible.

Frightened beyond words, no one dared to talk. That was when they heard something: footsteps. Someone was running on the beach, and then the sound shifted as if it were coming from the woods. Everybody frantically gathered their things and climbed into their car. Screams swirled all around them.

Adam took the wheel. When they were about to reach the lane, they saw a woman standing a few meters in front of the vehicle. It was the same woman they had seen earlier. They froze. He didn't want to drive further and close the distance between them and the strange woman. Suddenly, there was a loud bang! Something hit the car. Everyone instinctively looked behind them. Nothing was there.

When the driver looked forward, the woman was not in front of the car anymore. She was standing just outside the driver's door. It was dark, and he couldn't see the woman's face. He let out a scream and tried to drive away. The car choked! He turned the key, frantically. As soon as the engine revved back to life, he drove away as fast as he could. When they reached the main road, everyone sighed in relief.

They reached the edge of town just as the car broke down. The South African couple and Adam's mom walked the rest of the way while he and his now-sober dad stayed behind to watch the car. His mom called a friend of his dad's to pick them up and tow their car. They got home around 11:30 in the evening.

After sitting down to coffee, they told the family friend about what had just happened. He confirmed that they weren't the only ones who had experienced something horrific in that place. Flic en Flac was haunted, and many visitors had seen the woman in white.

While they escaped this traumatic experience relatively unscathed, there were others before them who hadn't been so lucky. People had actually died there. Stories of people being hypnotized, walking towards the sea in a trance, and never coming back were aplenty. Some say they were hurt by things being thrown at them. There was even a pregnant woman a few weeks away from giving birth who lost her baby while visiting the haunted location. She was rushed to the hospital a few hours after seeing the woman in white and had to undergo emergency surgery. Unfortunately, the surgeons were unable to save the baby.

Adam later found out that there was a cemetery near the beach. The woman was probably walking to where she had finally been laid to rest, but—as Adam found out first hand—rest, she did not.

CHAPTER 17:

NASA'S COVER-UPS

NASA's constant cover-ups and reluctance to talk about alien life provides many controversies among people. Their attitude led many to believe that there are alien creatures that wonder the soil of Earth and space sometimes. These people also believe that NASA knows more than it admits.

We already mentioned their unwillingness to share with the public the complete experience of Neil Armstrong and Apollo 11 crew, so it is no surprise that later NASA missions were also not fully reported back to the public.

The Apollo 14 mission of 1971 saw astronaut Dr. Mitchell being launched to space, or more precisely to the moon. Mitchell, himself stated that he had encountered aliens' multiple times, but NASA would always keep it to themselves. According to Mitchell, he was not the only one, but that also other NASA space employees witnessed seeing an unusual creature here and then as well. The aliens they saw were small and looked nothing like people.

Many praised their technology, which is superior to human inventions according to testimonials. The Roswell alien story of 1947 is also believed to be real, but exactly because of the technology, the USA government decided not to talk about the event in real terms, hoping to get a technological advantage over the then-enemy Soviet Union. The two world powers, caught in the Cold War, were constantly competing against each other in all aspects, military development, technological inventions, the space race, etc.

Dr. Mitchell's statements were denounced by NASA, which modestly stated not to be tracking foreign objects and aliens and that they do not keep anything secret. If this is true, can anyone explain why the live feed of the International Space Station is cut off when objects are roaming in space? This is yet another hint that the NASA might be playing games with people's minds trying to divert them from the path of the truth.

The Men in Black

The Men in Black, as he has become to be known, is a silencer of UFO and alien witnesses. One of the most astonishing stories is when he paid a visit to the hobby-UFO expert Dr. Hopkins, a well-reputed physician who reported being visited by this mysterious figure. According to the physician's story, he studied a UFO phenomenon in 1976, when he was given a call from a man allegedly from the UFO organization, who suddenly appeared at his home immediately after the phone call. He simply appeared out of nowhere in the middle of the room, without knocking, wearing a black hat and black tie. The man was also described as bold, short of eyelashes and eyebrows.

The man ordered him with a machine voice to end his UFO study and get rid of all evidence he gathered. The man left afterward by saying that his energy was running low. The very bizarre event is not the only one; other people have also reported strange visitor similarly dressed who threatened them. The threats led many to believe that there is a big secret being hidden from the global population and that alien existence is still a puzzle because the government and NASA keep the evidence out of reach and shut down people who talk about it.

The Roswell Incident

Everyone has heard of Roswell and the metal object that became known as UFO that was detected in Roswell in 1947. That was the first incident that would puzzle masses for decades, even today the story remains a big controversy. The story of the government simply does not add up to the facts and what many Roswell inhabitants have seen.

The US military first reported it was a flying disk just to change their story stating it was a weather balloon. The story was revived in the 1970s when the question of alien existence was raised again. Various conspiracy theories rose to fame which made the world doubt the government and NASA. Statistics has also shown that over 70% of people believe that the government conspired to hide true evidence and the Roswell alien landing on Earth.

Former Canadian Prime Minister Paul Hellyer also once stated that the US Government is using alien technology. He even argued that the government built identical flying saucers. The former minister deeply believes that UFOs are real and that their existence should not be denied.

Donna Hare is yet another individual who came in touch with NASA working as a contractor. She accidently discovered that NASA pictures are being "brushed up" before shown to the public. She once was shown a photo of the Earth shot from space where craft shadows were clearly visible and then she was told that the photos were airbrushed before release.

People who have something to say concerning their UFO research or alien experience are being controlled by the Air Force. For example, in 1947, a man shot a strange object with his camera in Arizona. After the photo had been published in the newspapers, the man was confronted by the Air Force which persuaded him to hand over the negatives, which they never returned.

UFO specialist, Keyhole was once a guest on a TV show to talk about UFOs. Well, the ufologist was censored and not allowed to talk freely. Every time he said something that was not approved by the station (read: by the Air Force), the sound was cut. Many believe that Keyhole was about to spill the beans about military studies on UFOs unknown to the public, which indicated that UFOs can move from planet to planet. Nevertheless, Keyhole was told by the TV station to stick to security standards after all.

CHAPTER 18:
CREDIBLE EYEWITNESS ACCOUNTS

In the 1960s, the Alien topic was hotter than ever, and Frank Drake, who was an astronomer, put together an equation which was supposed to calculate the probability of alien existence. To get the results, he focused on the number of life-supporting planets, and how many of them can host intelligent life. The equation came forth, it was estimated that there are hundreds of planets that exist and that communication from other planets could possibly be picked up.

There are some creepy stories about foreign object encounters dating back to the 1960s. Some of them are very bizarre, like the case of White and McDivitt. White and McDivitt, both astronauts, experienced a strange encounter with an odd metal object that appeared to have long arms. The event happened when they were traveling in a spacecraft back in 1965 over Hawaii. Unfortunately, the pictures that

McDivitt took failed to capture what was really going on and what they really saw. McDivitt also made a video of the incident, but for some reason was never released.

In 1969, Neil Armstrong and his fellow Apollo 11 astronaut Buzz Aldrin reported to have seen aliens, as they visited the moon. NASA tried to keep it secret, but the information busted when the communication between the astronauts and the base was published.

The communication was interrupted several times, but fear and disbelief could be felt in the conversation. Other spaceships are mentioned in the conversation as well, including visitors that were found on the Moon. Armstrong let the Mission Control know that two large objects were present and watched them.

Both astronauts reported that they were asked to leave. Armstrong recalled that their spaceships were superior to the Apollo 11's. NASA never revealed the official data due to fear of mass panic on Earth if faced with the knowledge of such an extraordinary encounter. Hysteria would have broken out all over the world if it were made public. Still, some information leaked which resulted in many UFO fanatics who try all in their power to prove their belief in aliens. Well, they are not far away, since evidence is piling up supporting the alien theory supporters.

Dancing Moon

In 1953 a professors and students at the College Campus in Tennessee spotted two strange objects in the sky. They said the objects resembled a moon and a star. The two objects were moving back and forth alternatively, increasing and decreasing in size, it lasted for half an hour. There is no explanation for what the professors and students witness that day.

Airplanes and UFO encounters

Another phenomenon that keeps the world wondering is the frequent case of airplanes almost clashing with UFOs. A similar encounter was reported by a veteran pilot, who stated to have spotted something like a delta-shaped object which was heading towards their direction. The pilot tried to go around the object to avoid a disaster, but suddenly right in front of the pilots eyes the craft disappeared.

Meteorites

Scientist Hoover, an astrobiologist claimed to have found an alien bug fossil in a meteorite. After running exhausting lab tests, the results he got are quite astonishing. Namely, he could not identify the fossil as an organism deriving from Earth. Whatever it was, it was extraterrestrial. The fossil lacked nitrogen and that they got stuck to the meteor due to contact with water. All that took place prior to the meteor landing on Earth. This is also clearly a sign that we are not alone on Earth and that we share the air with extraterrestrial beings that come and go. Many also believe that they watch over us and observe us.

The Wow Signal

The Wow Signal was detected in 1977 during the SETI (Search for Extraterrestrial Intelligence) project, when astronomer Jerry R. Ehman, who was a volunteer back then, discovered an equation that left him and his colleagues in shock. The equation suggested that they have picked up communication with extraterrestrial beings or signals. Before the project started, it was suggested that if there were any other living beings and intelligent civilizations that communicate via radio signals, they would also do it at a 1420mH frequency that is emitted by widespread hydrogen. The equation read as 6EQUJ5, and for many years it was believed that it enclosed a message.

The signal was coming from approximately 220 million light years away, and it was too strong to have been picked up with no advanced technology from "the other side." Still, even if no one ever came up with strong evidence that the signal was coming from aliens from another planet, many believe that it is exactly that.

2.1. Four Places Where Aliens Could Be Living

There are billions of galaxies and planets, and some are believed to support life. In the past, some of the places like Planet Mars were considered "dead" and not suitable for harboring any life form. Meanwhile, scientists have concluded that some places, Mars included, are probably inhabited or could be inhabited by a certain form of life. What places are believed to support life are listed below.

Mars

The possibility of life on Mars was discovered in the 19th and 20th century. Namely, channels that were spotted on Mars where believed to have been created by Mars inhabitants. Still, the theory was dropped after NASA's Mars missions during the 60s and 70s of the 20th century. The missionaries only found an empty landscape with no indicators of civilization. Still, some are very positive that life on Mars is possible since Mars has 2% of water. NASA data also indicate that life on Mars was even more supported billions of years ago when the planet was warmer and contained more water.

Titan

Titan is Saturn's largest moon and is the most similar place on Earth where hydrocarbon lakes can be found. Scientists speculated that there was also a handful quantity of water-ammonium within the oily lakes. Scientists think that there could be organisms that could adapt to such a habitat.

Enceladus

Enceladus is also one of Saturn's moons, on which an oceanic subsurface was discovered beneath a frozen surface. Scientists also agreed that the "trapped" water could be studied without breaking its crusty surface. The crust is estimated to be 40 km deep. When NASA sent their spacecraft, it discovered 101 water vapor and ice geysers which possibly emerge from the moon's south pole.

Europa

Since water represents the major source of life, and Europa seems to be the richest in water if compared to the above three places, scientists are positive that this place has the highest likeliness to support life. Europa is a moon of Jupiter and also has an icy surface, but researchers believe that plenty of water lures under the crust.

Even the government was intrigued by the discovery, so it funded $15 million to NASA for a mission to Europa. The NASA team already took action and is examining the state of play on the moon of Jupiter.

CHAPTER 19:
AN ENCOUNTER DOWN UNDER

This famous story of a UFO encounter and subsequent alien abduction has reportedly taken place in the foothills of the Dandenong mountain ranges, close to Belgrave, Victoria, Australia. Belgrave is a suburban settlement just east of Melbourne.

While this is certainly a fascinating story, it was not an incident that was witnessed and documented by thousands of people. As such, it has proven difficult to prove and has thus been vulnerable to harsh skepticism. The fact also is that the story was never disproven either and, in fact, the testimony has influenced numerous works in popular culture, such as some episodes of the famed X-Files.

The account was given by a Victorian woman called Kelly Cahill, who was twenty-seven at the time of her encounter, which happened in August of 1993. The mother of three was in a car that was being driven by her husband as the couple was making their way home after a visit to a friend's house late at night. Not far in the distance ahead of them, they saw a peculiar, glowing object hovering in the air. The craft was described as having an oval shape to it and what appeared to be windows all the way around. The UFO also boasted lights of a few different colors, with the windows glowing in orange.

These details became clear only when the car managed to catch up to the object and get closer for a better look. At that point, Kelly was certain that she saw dark silhouettes in the windows, moving around inside the mysterious aircraft. As Kelly began pointing this out to her husband, the UFO quickly dashed away to their left side and disappeared into the night, leaving the couple dumbfounded as to what had just happened.

They kept driving through the dark, determined to get home, but less than a mile down the road, they found themselves flashed by an incredibly strong, blinding light that lit up the whole area. Kelly's shock was immense, but short-lived because the strangest thing happened within moments. She remembered suddenly feeling much calmer and more composed as if nothing had happened, and she later described how it seemed to her that the car had traveled a considerable distance since the flash, yet the couple had no recollection of traversing that distance. The light was gone, and everything seemed to be back to normal. Kelly asked her husband if she had lost consciousness, but he too was confused.

That should have been the end of it, but once they made it back to the safety of their home, other strange things were noticed by Kelly. For one, she remembered noticing a very unpleasant smell resembling that of vomit, and an overwhelming feeling came over her, making her feel as though she was missing some time after the flash.

Even stranger was the unknown mark that Kelly said to have noticed on her navel that night. It was a very geometrical triangle that looked like a branding of some sort, and she was positive that she never had any kind of mark there before. To make matters worse, she told of how she was constantly suffering from strong stomach aches, uterine infections, and other gynecological issues, for which she had to be hospitalized a couple of times.

Those who are familiar with alien abduction cases know that there are a few of them where the victim reported similar experiences of inexplicable loss of time and memory. In many instances, these individuals undergo hypnosis to try and pluck the pieces of what may have happened to them deep from their brains, which is how they begin recollecting the specific circumstances of their actual abduction.

In Kelly Cahill's case, however, the memories started coming back on their own after a while. The first thing she remembered was that she saw a hovering UFO in a field on the side of the road, measuring about 150 feet wide. As it turns out, she and her husband pulled over and proceeded to investigate the craft, at which point they saw another car stop just up the road from them. Encouraged, the two kept walking forward to get a better look.

When they stopped to observe the hovering UFO from a shorter but still safe distance, it wasn't long until they saw a tall, dark creature appear right under the middle of the aircraft. Right behind this creature, seven or eight similar beings appeared as well. Kelly reported being overcome with an inexplicable, extraordinary feeling of dread that shook her to the core, leading her to scream. The creatures seemed to react to this and, as Kelly further explained, their eyes all lit up in red.

The way she described these dark creatures was particularly interesting. They were taller than the average human, and their darkness wasn't the kind brought about by a color. Rather, Kelly described the aliens as being without any color at all and almost without matter itself.

The expeditionary team of aliens then started to head straight toward them, with a smaller group splitting off and going for the occupants of the other car that had stopped to investigate. Soon thereafter, Kelly remembers passing out and waking up on the grass a bit closer to the road after that.

Sometime after this incident, Kelly got in touch with UFO investigators who investigated the case and conducted research with the occupants of the other car as well. As it turns out, Jane, Glenda, and Bill corroborated with a majority of what Kelly reported. They also drew sketches of the craft and the alien creatures, which were all very similar to what Kelly saw as well.

How much of the story is true remains a debated topic, but Kelly's account is one of the favorites among many UFO researchers. The descriptions of the beings that operated the UFO were very similar to other theories and reports that concern certain "shadow people" as a form of aliens that other people have allegedly encountered in the past. Some have suggested that these beings are not visitors from another planet, but rather they are creatures that intrude upon us from a different dimension.

CHAPTER 20:

THE MOST FAMOUSLY HAUNTED HOUSE IN ENGLAND

There is something about the land of England that makes one easily believe in stories of ghosts and spirits haunting its many old houses, castles, pubs and inns. Perhaps it is the antiquity of the land which has seen various legends grow around the people who have inhabited this ancient nation down the years. From the Old Saxon legends and the stories surrounding the Norman invasion to the marauding Vikings and the glory days of the British Empire, England has been fertile ground for ghosts to abound-if at all they needed fertile ground that is.

Strewn across this land are monuments that range from the thousands of year's old Stonehenge structures and Roman ruins from the times of Julius Caesar to hundreds of ancient and medieval castles, monasteries, palaces, grand houses, churches and cemeteries. Many of these structures are reportedly haunted by the people associated with them in the past; something that one can easily believe given how old some of these structures are.

Borley Rectory was a rather pretty Victorian mansion in the rather sparse surroundings of the village of Borley, Eastern Essex in England, which was gutted in a terrible fire that occurred in rather strange circumstances in the year 1939. However it shot to fame not on account of its status as a sterling example of Victorian architecture, but something very sinister and downright scary.

This goes back to the 1860s when the house pretty much stood tall in all its Gothic majesty. People from the area began to talk in hushed tones about hearing the sound of strange footsteps coming from the house in the dead of night. Far worse were accounts of a series of hair raising sightings- the ghost of a nun walking about the house, invisible beings ringing the bell to summon servants, a phantom carriage rushing onto the grounds and even two headless horsemen. Other reports talked about invisible beings hurling bottles!

Imagine how terribly scary it must have been in that far off place in the countryside with the mists rolling in and wolves and jackals baying in the distance and the rectory glowing softly in the moonlight or barely visible as a faint silhouette under a starry night. Add to that the antics of the spirits and you can imagine that it would take a very brave person indeed to stand his or her ground in such dire circumstances!

As was to be expected, given the extent of haunting reported from there, the reputation of Borley Rectory as a hotbed of paranormal activity earned it nationwide notoriety. So much so that the place was investigated by renowned paranormal expert Harry Price. So convinced was he of the house being severely haunted that he wrote two books on the subject! As often happens with accounts of places that are the scene of intense paranormal activity, the widespread publicity received by Borley Rectory led to a strong reaction from sceptics with the Society of Psychical Research casting grave doubts about the reported sightings and indeed on Price's credibility itself.

However, interest in the story hasn't waned in the story in all the years gone by, with the BBC even commissioning a documentary, which ultimately wasn't broadcast due to the possibility of the widow of the last rector to have lived in the house filing a lawsuit. There are many who attribute the sightings to the goings on at a Benedictine monastery that used to exist in the area in the fourteenth century. According to the legend a monk from the monastery had an affair with a nun from a nearby monastery which, as is usually the outcome in such cases, was soon discovered. The most severe punishment was visited upon the unfortunate pair with the former being burnt at the stake and the latter walled up alive within the convent.

The rectory had been ordered built by the pastor of the Borley Church, Rev. Henry Bull in 1862 on land that the locals believed was haunted and soon enough there were sightings of ghosts including the long dead nun reported by the pastor, his family and servants. They also heard the footsteps in the middle of the night, as also the rapping sounds that would disturb their sleep in the house.

However what they experienced was not as terrifying and intimidating as what the last parson of the church and resident of the rectory, Rev. Lionel Foyster and his wife Marianne Foyster faced. The latter in fact reported a whole series of terrifying incidents that included messages scribbled on the wall, the couple's daughter getting inexplicably locked up in a room, the window panes being smashed and Marianne even on occasions being violently thrown off her bed.

Their daughter Adelaide once reported being viciously attacked by a terrifying supernatural being and Lionel himself was once hit with a large stone when he tried exorcism to force the spirits out of the house. Living at Borley Rectory proved to be more than Lionel Foyster could take and he soon became quite sick as a result of which the Foysters moved out after spending some five years there.

After their departure, Harry Price entered into a yearlong lease agreement with the owners of the rectory and had college students and others spend weekends there observing any occurrence of supernatural phenomenon. One of the observers, a young woman by the name of Helen Glanville claimed to have met the ghost of the Marie the nun who had been murdered in the rectory for the sin of having had an affair. She was the one who would be scribbling messages on the wall asking for help.

Helen also reported meeting the ghost of a man by the name of Sunex Amures who had apparently informed her that he would set fire to the rectory on 27th March 1938 at precisely 9 pm and that at the end of it all there would be the discovery of the bones of a person who had been murdered there. Apparently, that is precisely what happened when the accidental knocking down of a lamp by the new owner of the rectory, a Captain Gregson, started the fire that razed the building. As predicted the bones of a young woman were discovered in the ruins, which were duly accorded a Christian burial in the Liston Churchyard.

In the decades since the rectory burnt down, there have been many attempts to try and rationalize the sighting of paranormal phenomena at the site by doubting the veracity of Harry Price's accounts and even the motives behind Lionel and Marianne Foyster's accounts. It is all very well in today's times when even the burnt out ruins of the rectory have been demolished to try and scientifically analyze paranormal phenomena that occurred so many years ago by people who are no longer alive to defend their version, but to those who experienced the hauntings at Borley rectory, it was all very real indeed.

But for nearly eighty years there were bone chilling stories that emerged from the profoundly mysterious Borley rectory which riveted the people like nothing else before, so much so that the place was referred to as the most haunted house in England. Believe you me that is no mean reputation to possess!

One often wonders how people continue to live or stay on in a house where they have experienced the supernatural. Most people I know wouldn't stay a moment longer than necessary in such a place. Perhaps a supernatural encounter is not as bizarre as it might seem to those of us who haven't experienced it. Maybe there is some sort of an epiphany brought on by the experience which makes us realize that we are in contact with a kindred soul that was once flesh and bone like us!

CHAPTER 21:

THE PHOENIX LIGHTS

It really is amazing that an event so clear, so enormous, and witnessed and documented by so many people can remain such a mystery. The world of the UFO phenomenon is filled to the brim with such incidents, however, and the famous mass sighting of 1997 in Phoenix, Arizona is precisely one such case.

This sighting occurred quite some time before access to advanced editing software, and other computer technology became widespread and, the witnesses, photographs, and videos are plentiful and clear enough.

Although the encounters were named after the city of Phoenix, the event occurred over a much larger area that included Arizona and Nevada, with some reports even coming out of New Mexico. The events of that night on March 13 began to unfold at around 6:55 PM, when an individual in Henderson, Nevada encountered the first UFO, setting in motion a string of escalating sightings that would go on for hours thereafter.

As he reported, the man saw a large, V-shaped craft swoop in and head directly toward him, passing over his head to the southeast. He described the unidentified object as being roughly the size of a Boeing 747 airliner, having six bright lights at its tip and producing a whooshing noise that resembled a strong wind.

Another one of the initial sightings was reported above the Superstition Mountains close to Phoenix around 7:30, where witnesses explained they saw mysterious lights in the sky. Another sighting occurred around 8:15 when a retired police officer observed five light sources flying in formation.

Around that time, hundreds of reports started coming into the emergency services, media outlets, the National UFO Reporting Center, and many other organizations from many different locations around Phoenix. The reports described all sorts of different anomalies in the sky, including various objects, flight patterns, a wide range of colors, and crafts of all sizes. Whatever was taking place was either huge or the mysterious flying objects was so fast that it flew over the state of Arizona with ease and within minutes.

North of Phoenix, multiple witnesses reported seeing an enormous object, much like the one that was seen in Henderson sometime before that. There were five lights seen in the sky, but the witnesses concluded that a single object was in question because it blocked a part of the night's starry sky, making it clear that this was a big, dark aircraft. There were no erratic maneuvers or any sudden moves, and the aircraft instead just glided casually overhead and disappeared into the distance.

Another object was spotted by a family, coming in from Camelback Mountain, Arizona and hovering for several minutes over their heads. This UFO too was large and overshadowing a large portion of the sky, but its appearance was somewhat different. As the UFO continued to hover over them, they were able to make out its actual structure, eye witness also noticed that the rear of the craft was slightly lite up. After remaining idle for some time, the aircraft began to move in the direction of the Sky Harbor International Airport, as its lights grew dim and it disappeared. And sure enough, the UFO was then reported by the air traffic control tower personnel and numerous pilots.

Flocks of lights, large V-shaped UFOs, and various other anomalies continued to be witnessed all over the state of Arizona, cities such as Scottsdale, Gilbert, Glendale, Casa Grande, and quite a few others all reported seeing a similar object. At the peak of UFO activity, the most diverse of reports continued to pour in, causing a lot of confusion and disorientation both for law enforcement and the National UFO Reporting Center. The two most common versions of the UFOs appeared to be either that of a large craft looming overhead or multiple lights flying in formation, not seeming to be part of one whole. Reports of giant motherships that were V-shaped aircrafts and were splitting into multiple objects were also being called in. It was estimated later that some of the witnessed "motherships" would have been up to a mile wide.

Things took a rather interesting turn a few hours after the mass sightings had subsided. Namely, the National UFO Reporting Center received a call at around 3:20 in the morning from a man claiming to be serving in the Air Force, stationed during that time at the Luke Air Force Base, west of Phoenix. The man said that the USAF sent out two fighter jets from that very base to try and intercept the UFOs, which they did. He provided intricate details in his story, a lot of which seemed to be logical and fitting into the larger picture as the investigators later found. The mysterious man placed yet another call to the Center a couple of days later, simply stating that he was being assigned far away in Greenland.

During the incidents on the night in question, a particularly eerie account was given by a group of individuals north of Phoenix. These people, who were real estate agents, explained that they too had a very close encounter with an enormous alien mothership. They further went on to say that they estimated the spacecraft to be up to a mind-boggling two miles in width. As the ship loomed over an area very close to Phoenix, these witnesses described seeing the object only dimly lit along its edge, with light apparently emanating from the inside. They believed to be looking at a long, windowed area on the craft, and they reported seeing silhouettes of shadowy figures inside the aircraft.

Another highly intriguing report came from a truck driver who described his witnessing of the military's involvement in the incident. He was on his way to a plant near the Luke AFB from Camp Verde. The man described that as he drove down the road, he was constantly stalked by two UFOs for at least a couple of hours. When he arrived at the plant, the two mysterious crafts proceeded to just hover not far from there. He described the UFOs as two brightly glowing orbs.

He further reported that three fighter jets were quickly scrambled from the base to investigate the unidentified crafts. However, as soon as they came in close contact with the UFOs, they rapidly gained altitude and just vanished. It was reported that a serviceman from the Luke AFB later corroborated the driver's story to the National UFO Reporting Center.

Between 9:30 and 10:00 PM of that eventful night was when one of the most prominent pieces of footage was recorded.

Among the many recordings and photographs, this is one of the clearest bits of video that continues to be among the first pieces of evidence that people turn to when examining this famous case. The footage shows a formation of lights just south of Phoenix, some of which appear to vanish and reappear multiple times.

This footage is also among the most discussed evidence concerning the case, and it was such in the immediate aftermath of the incident as well. This was when theories began to be consolidated and possible explanations offered, the weakest of which probably came from the authorities themselves.

Through the Public Affairs Office of the Luke Air Force Base, the military attempted to brush the incident off by explaining that the lights were nothing more than flares dropped from one of their aircrafts during a routine training mission at around 10 PM that night. This answer has next to no merit because it doesn't account for sightings prior to that time, the behavior of the many objects that were seen, and the large area from which the thousands of reports emerged.

The Governor of Arizona, Fife Symington himself reported being a witness to the strange lights, although he stood by the official explanation provided by the military. However, sometime later, the man himself admitted that the investigation was less than convincing and that he believed the objects to have not been of this world.

As it turned out just recently in 2017, there was another prominent witness to the anomalies of that night, and it was none other than the famed actor Kurt Russell. As he told in an interview to the BBC, he happened to be piloting an airplane in the area that night, when he personally witnessed six unidentified lights flying over Phoenix.

Although the media seemed to all but ignore this major incident at the time, the story did gain traction a couple of months later in numerous newspapers. However, the apparent lack of live media coverage as the events unfolded over a multiple-hour period that night is strange indeed, not to say suspicious. With or without the media, though, the infamous Phoenix Lights UFO case has cemented its place not just in the UFO enthusiast circles but also in popular culture, remaining one of the most discussed phenomena in its field to this very day.

CHAPTER 22:

TRAVAILS OF THE PERRON FAMILY

The case of the Perron Family haunting achieved celebrity status thanks to the super success of the Warner Bros movie The Conjuring which was largely based on the experiences of this hapless family. The Perron's lived for a decade in a very old house that apparently was home to an unusually large number of spirits of some of its old residents, who though long dead, never left home. It, therefore, fell to the lot of the Perron family to experience the strangest, most bizarre and terribly frightening paranormal phenomena in the years they spent in absolute misery and terror in the company of beings who were not from the world of the living.

The Persons were a large and happy family comprising of Roger Perron, wife Carolyn Perron, and their five young pretty daughters Andrea, Nancy, Christine, Cynthia and April, when they had chanced upon what appeared to them just the right home that the family needed-the picturesque

Arnold Estate in Harrisville, Rhode Island. Their troubles with the world of spirits started soon after they bought and moved into, what had appeared to be a lovely country house in the midst of sprawling two hundred acres of land in the year 1970.

Unknown to them at the time of the purchase, the property had a checkered and violent history with many of its old residents, as well as other people from the area, having met with violent ends there. The Perrons, especially the children soon became aware of the presence of a number of spirits, not all of whom were particularly unpleasant, though. There was, however, one particular spirit with a horribly wicked persona who was particularly vicious to Carolyn Perron and made her years in the house excruciatingly painful.

What the children experienced were random nightly disturbances like furniture being dragged across the floor, doors being slammed shut or chillingly even a small child's voice call out for its mother all night long. Though these spirits apparently didn't cause any harm or danger, the impact it must have had on the fragile psyche of small children can be well imagined.

The one who tormented Carolyn was purportedly a practicing witch Bathsheba Sherman who had lived next to the Perron Family home on what was known as the Sherman Farm in the 1800s. Apparently she had had four children, none of whom survived beyond seven years of age, which made the people of the area believe that she had sacrificed her own children to the Devil.

An investigation was ordered into the death of an infant son of hers who it was suspected was done to death by Bathsheba with a sewing needle. No conclusive case however was made out and she was let off. It was the spirit of this person who the Perrons believed had committed suicide by hanging herself from a rafter in their house that had deviously targeted Carolyn with the intent of driving her off the property.

The most frightening instance of this was experienced when she was once woken up by a frightening looking old woman, her head hanging to the side, warning her to leave the house or she would unleash death and misery on her. This and other instances of severe harassment that included levitating beds and other household objects, as well as weird night long noises made Carolyn's life a nightly hell of unending misery.

The highly concerned Perrons decided to seek the help of celebrated paranormal investigator couple Ed and Lorraine Warren who surmised that it was indeed the vile and vicious spirit of Bathsheba who was tormenting Carolyn. Unfortunately, their presence only made matters worse for the Perrons, with the evil spirit in question apparently getting enraged and deciding to worsen matters by invading Carolyn's body and possessing it.

The Perron family requested the famed investigators to leave, as they weren't really helping matters. Bathsheba did apparently relent after that and left Carlyn's body, but the haunting of the family continued right till the time that they left the property. Financial constraints had apparently prevented the family from selling the property all those many years. Finally, in 1980, they were in a position to sell the property and make a move to far off Georgia where the finally got rid of the spirits that bothered them, apparently not entirely by some accounts.

The saga of the Perron family haunting has captured public imagination like nothing else, and the Hollywood movie is proof of that. Not everyone is convinced of the truth of this riveting tale with many attributing motives to the Perron family as well as the Warrens. Some point to the fact that a Pastor's family who lived on the supposedly haunted property reported no abnormal experiences in their time there. The supporters of the Perrons and Warrens though claim that the fact that a man of God lived there explained the absence of any paranormal activity.

The current owners of the property though deny that there is any paranormal activity happening upon the property even though they admit having a couple of odd experiences. In fact so hassled are they at the media and public attention surrounding their home thanks to the movie that they have contemplated legal action against Warner Bros.

The Perrons though steadfastly maintain that the terrible hauntings they experienced are a fact with their daughter, Andrea, even writing a book, House of Darkness: House of Light about the strange and terribly frightening experience, she and her family endured in their now infamous Rhode Island Home. The thing about paranormal experiences is that you have to have undergone one to know it is real. If you haven't, you can conjecture about it, but never know the truth of its occurrence. But do you have the right to be judgmental about it, even though you don't have the faintest idea about what it entails? You dear reader be the judge of that.

CONCLUSION

If you've gone through all these stories you're probably feeling a bit creeped out...right?

The idea behind this book isn't necessary to scary you but to open a window to other possibilities and perspectives. To look within yourself and maybe to ask yourself deeper questions.

Are ghost real?

Are we alone hear in this vast universe?

Despite all stories and evidence, many still refuse the idea of the paranormal and find it ridiculous. Still, when we consider how big the world let alone the Universe is, it is quite likely there are strange anomalies out there that are unexplainable.

Hopefully, this book will cause you to ask more questions about our purpose in this universe. You can take what you like, and discard what you do not, but let´s agree on one thing. Our brain cannot keep rationalizing everything that we experience. Some things simply have no logical explanation. Thank you again for reading Paranormal Horror Stories